"Tell me something, Russ. Do you wear boxers or briefs?"

"Pardon me?" He felt himself blush. Surely he'd heard wrong.

"I have this theory. Men who wear briefs are your garden-variety uptight conservatives. Men who play by the rules, never take risks and have little sense of humor. They are judgmental, restrained and controlling. I figure it has something to do with briefs cutting off the blood flow to the brain."

Russ wished desperately that beneath his stiff, perfectly creased uniform was a pair of paisley silk boxers. "You're crazy," he scoffed.

She grinned triumphantly. "You're definitely a briefs man, Russ." And she was going to enjoy finding out just how badly he wanted to change....

Dear Reader,

What a month of wonderful reading Romance has for you! Our FABULOUS FATHERS title, *Most Wanted Dad,* continues Arlene James's miniseries THIS SIDE OF HEAVEN. Single dad and police officer Evans Kincaid can't quite handle his daughter's wild makeup and hairdos. Luckily—or not so luckily—the pretty lady next door is full of advice....

Do You Take This Child? is the last book of Marie Ferrarella's THE BABY OF THE MONTH CLUB miniseries—and our BUNDLES OF JOY title. Any-minute-mom-to-be Dr. Sheila Pollack expects to raise her baby all alone. But when the *long-absent* dad-to-be suddenly bursts into the delivery room, Sheila says "I do" between huffs and puffs!

In *Reilly's Bride* by Patricia Thayer, Jenny Murdock moves to Last Hope, Wyoming, to escape becoming a bride. But the town's crawling with eligible bachelors who want wives. So why isn't she happy when she falls for the one man who doesn't want to walk down the aisle?

Carla Cassidy continues THE BAKER BROOD miniseries with *Mom in the Making.* Single dad Russ Blackburn's little son chases away every woman who comes near his dad. It just figures the boy would like Bonnie Baker—a woman without a shred of mother material in her!

And don't miss the handsome drifter who becomes a woman's birthday present in Lauryn Chandler's *Her Very Own Husband,* or the two adorable kids who want their parents together in Robin Nicholas's *Wrangler's Wedding.*

Enjoy!

Melissa Senate,
Senior Editor

Please address questions and book requests to:
Silhouette Reader Service
U.S.: 3010 Walden Ave., P.O. Box 1325, Buffalo, NY 14269
Canadian: P.O. Box 609, Fort Erie, Ont. L2A 5X3

MOM IN THE MAKING

Carla Cassidy

Silhouette
R O M A N C E™
Published by Silhouette Books
America's Publisher of Contemporary Romance

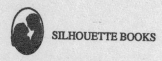

SILHOUETTE BOOKS

ISBN 0-373-19147-2

MOM IN THE MAKING

This edition published by arrangement with Harlequin Books S.A.

® and TM are trademarks of Harlequin Books S.A., used under license.
Trademarks indicated with ® are registered in the United States Patent
and Trademark Office, the Canadian Trade Marks Office and in other
countries.

Printed in U.S.A.

Books by Carla Cassidy

Silhouette Romance

Patchwork Family #818
Whatever Alex Wants... #856
Fire and Spice #884
Homespun Hearts #905
Golden Girl #924
Something New #942
Pixie Dust #958
The Littlest Matchmaker #978
The Marriage Scheme #996
Anything for Danny #1048
*Deputy Daddy #1141
*Mom in the Making #1147

Silhouette Desire

A Fleeting Moment #784
Under the Boardwalk #882

*The Baker Brood

Silhouette Shadows

Swamp Secrets #4
Heart of the Beast #11
Silent Screams #25
Mystery Child #61

Silhouette Intimate Moments

One of the Good Guys #531
Try To Remember #560
Fugitive Father #604

Silhouette Books

Silhouette Shadows Short Stories 1993
"Devil and the Deep Blue Sea"

The Loop
Getting it Right: Jessica

CARLA CASSIDY

is the author of ten young-adult novels, as well as many contemporary romances. She's been a cheerleader for the Kansas City Chiefs football team and has traveled the East Coast as a singer and dancer in a band, but the greatest pleasure she has had is in creating romance and happiness for readers.

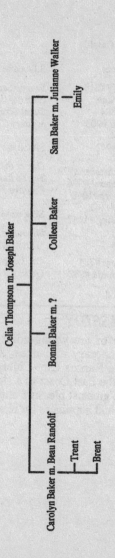

The Baker Brood

Celia Thompson m. Joseph Baker

Carolyn Baker m. Beau Randolf
Trent
Brent

Bonnie Baker m. ?

Colleen Baker

Sam Baker m. Julianne Walker
Emily

Chapter One

Bonnie Baker frowned and sighed as she saw the flashing red lights in her rearview mirror. She eased off the gas pedal and pulled the rental car over to the side of the road, braking to a stop in front of the Casey's Corners Hardware Store.

Terrific. She couldn't be more than a block or two away from her sister's house, and unless she was very lucky, she was about to eat another speeding ticket. Her third in the hundred-mile drive from the airport in Wichita.

She wouldn't have been speeding had there been a lot of traffic. The road was virtually deserted, and she'd allowed her need to get to her sister's house to overrule any speed limit. How was she supposed to know the state of Kansas had an abundance of good-ole-boy patrolmen who had nothing better to do than write speeding tickets?

She shut off the engine and waited for the officer to approach. Maybe she could tell him she was on her way to a funeral. No, he would never believe it at this time of night. She could tell him the truth—that she'd walked out in the middle of her wedding, suddenly confused and certain she was about to make a major mistake. She'd hopped on a jet and flown from Europe. Now she was jet-lagged and on the verge of cranky. No, she wasn't about to bare her soul to anyone.

Well, she could certainly tell him she was Carolyn's sister, and Carolyn was married to the sheriff of this little town. Hey, wouldn't it be funny if this was her introduction to her new brother-in-law? She grinned at the thought of him stopping her, the vision of another ticket usurped by the more pleasant image of a family reunion.

Straightening, she eyed the officer in her rearview mirror. If he was her brother-in-law, the first thing she needed to do was congratulate her sister on her taste. Tall and slim, he walked toward her car with a masculine stride that bespoke control and authority. Bonnie had always liked a man who took charge. She liked to make them crazy.

Darn. She couldn't remember her brother-in-law's name. When the letter had come from Carolyn announcing her marriage, Bonnie had been in Europe fighting the advances of an amorous prince.

Was the name Wade? No, that wasn't it, although Bonnie distinctly remembered reading that her sister had married a man with a good Southern name.

"License and registration, please."

She peered up at him. "Rhett?" she ventured. It was the only other Southern male name she could think of.

"Pardon me?"

He frowned, the gesture only intensifying his attractiveness. His face was lean, the only hint of softness a cleft in his chin.

"Are you Carolyn's husband?" Drat, what was the man's name?

"Carolyn? No, that's Beau. He's now the sheriff. I'm the new deputy sheriff. Now, can I see your license and registration?" He held out his hand.

Beau. Of course. Beau Randolf. Bonnie turned slightly in her seat, stuck her hand out the window and grabbed his. She shook it and turned on her million-watt smile. "Hi, I'm Bonnie Baker, Carolyn's sister. I didn't catch your name."

"I didn't mention it." He released her hand and opened a summons pad. "Are you going to hand over your license and registration, or am I going to have to write you up for being uncooperative?"

"I don't suppose you'd consider giving me a break instead of issuing me a ticket?" Bonnie widened her eyes, a look of innocence that usually garnered her what she wanted.

He shook his head. "It's not my job to give breaks."

Bonnie bit back a sharp retort and grabbed her purse off the seat next to her. What a jerk. She was just trying to be friendly. She extracted her wallet and withdrew her driver's license. "Are you sure my brother-in-law would approve of you giving his favorite relative a ticket?" she asked as she handed her license to him.

"In law enforcement there are no favorite relatives. There are only law-abiding citizens and lawbreakers."

Terrific. She had been pulled over by Robocop. She tapped a sculptured nail on the steering wheel.

He peered at the photo on her license, then her. "This doesn't look like you."

She shrugged. No matter how handsome he was, the man was definitely a jerk. "When that picture was taken I was going through a 'blondes have more fun' phase." She flipped a strand of her dark hair. "Since then I've gone back to my natural color."

"Natural is always better."

His dark eyes held the first hint of amusement. It rankled Bonnie. Sure he could afford to be amused now; he was about to write her up a ticket.

"Weren't you supposed to be in Europe getting married to some prince?" He leaned against the side of her car and gazed at her with unabashed curiosity.

Bonnie frowned. "How did you know that?"

He shrugged, and Bonnie couldn't help but notice the width of his shoulders. Jerks should never be hunks. It was so disconcerting.

"Carolyn mentioned it. I thought the wedding was yesterday. Spending separate honeymoons, you and the prince?"

"Of course not," she snapped. "I changed my mind and decided not to marry Prince Helmut."

His dark eyes flickered, and one corner of his mouth curved upward. "That was his name? No wonder you backed out. Who on earth would want to go through life as Mrs. Helmut?"

"That had nothing to do with it. Helmut is his first name, and it's a fine old French name." Bonnie certainly didn't want to discuss her personal life with this stranger, particularly the details of the disastrous wedding fiasco. "Look, are you going to write me a ticket or not? I've been traveling for the better part of the past twenty-four hours. I'm tired and cranky and all I want to do is get to Carolyn's house. By the way, can you tell me where Elm Street is?"

"It was the last street you zoomed by at sixty miles an hour in a twenty-five-mile-an-hour zone." He completed writing out the ticket and tore it from his pad. He handed it to her and looked at his watch. "If you'll follow me, I'll take you to Carolyn and Beau's place."

"That's not necessary," Bonnie protested as she threw the ticket over her shoulder into the back seat. She certainly didn't want any favors from him. "I wouldn't want to keep you from this important job of writing tickets to all the speeders who roar into town."

"Oh, I think it *is* necessary."

He shone his flashlight into the back seat, where the ticket he had just written snuggled against the two she'd received earlier in the evening.

"I always escort habitual offenders to their destination."

"Fine." Bonnie turned the key and started the engine. "Just take me to Carolyn's house, then get out of my life."

He grinned, suddenly devastatingly handsome as he doffed his hat.

"My pleasure, ma'am."

Bonnie rarely fought her impulses, but she did resist the urge to tromp on the gas pedal and peel rubber as she pulled away from the curb. Again she tapped a sculptured fingernail against the steering wheel as a sign of frustration while she waited for the police car to move in front of hers.

Terrific. Not only was she appearing at her sister's house broke and unexpected, but she also had a police escort. Bonnie grinned. Nobody could accuse her of not knowing how to make a grand entrance.

Five minutes later, she parked behind the police car in front of an attractive, older house. Caro's house. It was hard to believe her older sister was now married and the adoptive mother of year-old twin boys.

She got out of her car, gave the officer a jaunty salute, then groaned as he left his car and joined her on the sidewalk. "You don't have to be chivalrous. It isn't necessary for you to see me to the door," she told him.

He grinned. "Don't mistake me for a prince, sweetheart. I don't have a chivalrous bone in my body. I was just going inside to talk to Beau."

Bonnie blushed, irritation winging through her. "Well, pardon me, sweetheart. I thought you might be a gentleman, but obviously I was mistaken." Brushing past him, she strode up to the front door and rang the bell. The door opened immediately, and she grinned at her sister, whose eyes widened in surprise.

"Bonnie!" Carolyn squealed.

Throwing open the screen door, Carolyn grabbed Bonnie in a welcoming embrace. Bonnie felt a sudden sting of tears in her eyes as she allowed herself a moment in her sister's warm embrace.

Before the tears could fall, she pushed away and laughed in abandon. "Hey, no need to hug the stuffing out of me." She gave her sister a dazzling smile.

"What are you doing here? I thought you were getting married." She pulled Bonnie out of the doorway and into the living room, spying the officer behind Bonnie. "Russ, I didn't know you were out there, too. Beau is putting the kids to bed. He should be out in just a minute.'' She gestured toward the sofa. ''Well, come on, sit down both of you.''

Bonnie started toward the sofa, frowning as her shoulders bumped into Russ, who'd headed in the same direction. She stopped and glared at him. The man was obviously a barbarian. At least he'd had the manners to take off his hat. The thick, curly, dark hair that was revealed only added to his attractiveness.

''After you,'' he said, sweeping his hand in courtly fashion for her to precede him.

Instead of sitting on the sofa, Bonnie sank down onto one of the two easy chairs in the room, exhaustion returning full force.

''Where did you two meet up?'' Carolyn asked as she sat down on the sofa next to Russ.

''On Main Street. She was lost. Since I was getting off duty, I offered to escort her here,'' Russ explained.

''What luck.'' Carolyn beamed happily.

''Oh, yes, I'll be sure to include him when I count my blessings tonight,'' Bonnie returned dryly, although she was grateful he hadn't mentioned the speeding ticket.

She focused her attention on her sister. The last time she had seen Carolyn had been two months ago at their father's funeral. That was the last time the three Baker sisters had been together.

''You look good,'' Bonnie said to Carolyn. It was true. She appeared relaxed, at peace. She had a glow that Bonnie instantly envied, the glow of a woman who'd found the love of her life.

"I'm happy," Carolyn answered simply.

Again Bonnie felt a wistful arrow of envy shoot through her.

"Here's my better half now." Bonnie stood up as Caro's husband stepped into the room.

"This is Beau. Beau, this is Bonnie."

In three long strides he was across the room, grasping Bonnie's hand warmly. "It's nice to meet you. Carolyn has told me so much about you." He gazed at her curiously. "We thought you were in Europe preparing to marry some prince."

"Prince Helmut," Russ quipped.

Again Bonnie glared at him irritably. Why didn't he go home? There was something about his arrogant attractiveness that rattled her.

"I called off the wedding."

"Why?" Carolyn asked.

Beau released her hand, and Bonnie sank back down into the chair. "I was standing in the church in my wedding dress, the church was filled with guests, and I suddenly realized I couldn't go through with it." She shrugged, shoving away the memory of that horrible moment. She didn't want to think about that now. Grinning irreverently, she waved her hands to dismiss the entire topic. "I just wasn't ready to make a commitment to any one man. You know me, never in one place for long. But let's not talk about that. I want to hear all about those nephews of mine.''

"If you'll excuse us, Russ and I will just go out to the kitchen while you two talk babies,'' Beau said, motioning for Russ to follow him out of the room.

"He seems really nice,'' Bonnie said the moment the men had left.

"Russ is a terrific guy.''

Bonnie scowled. "I wasn't talking about him. I was talking about your husband.''

"Oh. Beau is the most wonderful man in the entire world,'' Carolyn agreed, her face once again lit up. "But Russ is wonderful, too. He's also very single.''

"I think he's a jerk!'' Bonnie exclaimed. "He gave me a speeding ticket.''

"Were you speeding?''

Bonnie smiled reluctantly. "Yes, I guess I was. But I still think he's a jerk.''

Carolyn laughed and leaned forward to clasp Bonnie's hand. "Oh, Bonnie, it's so good to have you here. So, what are your plans? How long can you stay?''

Bonnie shrugged. "I really don't have any plans. When things fell apart with the prince, I just hopped on a plane and decided to come here. Your letters made me fall half in love with Casey's Corners.''

"It's a great place to live,'' Carolyn stated. "But if you're looking for excitement, Casey's Corners, Kansas, is definitely not the place to be.''

"At the moment excitement is the last thing I'm looking for. I know I should have called first, but would you mind having some company for a couple weeks? Just until I decide what the next phase of my life is going to be."

Carolyn laughed again and squeezed Bonnie's hand. "Oh, Bonnie, I wouldn't have expected you to show up any other way but unexpectedly. Of course you can stay here. For as long as you want."

Bonnie sighed in relief, realizing she'd been half-afraid Caro would turn her away. After all, following their father's murder, Bonnie hadn't hung around to help with anything. Instead she'd run, trying to escape her grief and fear by spending money frivolously and partying frantically each night until dawn. It had been easier to stuff her pain beneath a frenzied life-style than to face it and deal with her demons.

"So, did you tell Bonnie that we have the smartest, most talented boys in the world?" Beau said as he and Russ reentered the living room.

Carolyn shook her head. "We didn't even get to the topic of the twins. We've got so much to catch up on."

Bonnie stifled a yawn with the back of her hand, then grinned ruefully. "Sorry, jet lag," she explained.

"It's late. We should all call it a night," Beau said. He smiled at Bonnie. "If you'll give me your keys, I'll get your bags from the car."

"I appreciate it. I'm so tired I can't think straight." Bonnie gave the keys to her brother-in-law. She studiously ignored Russ, even though she could feel his dark, disapproving gaze on her. Why was he hanging around? He looked at her as if she were a foreign species sent down to Earth to wreak havoc. She grinned inwardly. Caro had often accused her of that very thing.

"Bonnie, Russ has been staying with us while he house-hunts. He's sleeping in our spare room, so is it okay if we put you out here on the sofa? It pulls out into a bed," Carolyn said.

Bonnie looked at Russ half-expectantly. If he was any kind of gentleman at all, he would offer to take the sofa and give her the bedroom. Instead he smiled, a mocking, knowing grin, and made no offer to relinquish the bedroom.

He helped Carolyn move the coffee table and pull out the bed. Bonnie couldn't believe it. She would go to a motel, but she wasn't ready to confess to her sister that she'd spent her quarterly inheritance check in record time and was hopelessly broke, at least until the next check due her came in two months.

She met Beau at the door and helped him with her suitcases, blushing slightly as the evidence of her latest escapade—her discarded white frothy wedding dress—exploded out of the side zipper of one of the bags.

"Oh, Bonnie, how beautiful!" Carolyn exclaimed as she plucked the gown up from the floor where it had fallen and held it up in front of her.

"You can have it," she told her sister. "Maybe you and Beau can have another ceremony in a couple of years."

"Don't be silly," Carolyn protested. "We'll hang it in the closet, and it will be ready for you when you decide to get married. Who knows, maybe you'll be as lucky as me and find your Prince Charming right here in Casey's Corners."

Bonnie laughed. "Believe me, the last thing I want is a man in my life to stifle all my fun. Besides—" she shot a sidelong look at Russ "—if Officer Friendly here is a sample of the single men in town, I might decide to become a nun."

Russ laughed good-naturedly. "Ah, Princess, I have a feeling you'll be long gone from Casey's Corners before that happens." He turned to Beau and Carolyn. "I'll see you in the morning." Then he turned and disappeared down the hallway.

"That man..." Bonnie sputtered ineffectually. She grabbed the opposite corner of the sheet Carolyn was fitting over the sofa mattress.

"I think I'll go on to bed, too," Beau said.

"I'll be there in just a minute," Carolyn told him. He nodded and left the room. "Honey, go easy on Russ," Carolyn said to Bonnie. "He's been through a rough time. His wife left him a little over a year ago.''

"Hmm, I can understand that." Bonnie took the pillowcase Carolyn handed her, ignoring her sister's look of censure.

"He has an eight-year-old son and is trying to start fresh here. The boy is back in Chicago right now with Russ's mother. As soon as Russ gets settled in his own place he's sending for Daniel.''

"I'm sorry he's had a rough time, and I hope he'll be very happy here," Bonnie said grudgingly. "But that doesn't make me like him any better. He's arrogant and self-righteous and smug.''

"And I think you're overtired and overreacting." Carolyn leaned forward and kissed Bonnie on the cheek. "Get some sleep. We'll see if you don't think differently in the morning.''

"There aren't enough hours in the night to change my mind on that issue," Bonnie returned. She picked up her overnight bag. "If you'll just tell me where the bathroom is, I'll change into my pajamas and sleep off this jet lag. I'm sorry I'm so cranky, but you know I get this way when I travel long distances.''

Carolyn pointed down the hallway. "First door on the left.''

Bonnie nodded and headed for the bathroom, eager to change out of her wrinkled clothes and into her comfortable nightgown. She was so tired and knew the exhaustion was as much emotional as physical.

As she reached for the knob, the door flew open and Russ stepped out. It was obvious he had just showered. Droplets of water still clung to his hair and spiked his sinfully long eyelashes. He wore only a pair of jeans, which rode low on his lean hips. His chest was a magnificent display of bronzed muscle and swirling, dark hair. The man was an Adonis.

"Would you like for me to scrub your royal back?" he asked quietly.

His mocking smile shattered the fantasy image she'd just created. She smiled sweetly. "I would much prefer that you kiss my royal—"

"Bonnie," Carolyn interrupted, placing a steadying hand on Bonnie's shoulder. "The towels are under the sink and your bed is all ready."

Bonnie nodded and swallowed the last of her sentence.

"Good night, Carolyn. Sweet dreams, Princess," Russ said, brushing past Bonnie and out into the hallway.

"Sweet dreams to you, too," Bonnie murmured, wishing with all her might that he would dream of a beautiful princess knighting him over the head with a two-by-four.

Chapter Two

Russ Blackburn sat in the chair next to the sofa, staring at the woman who slept deeply. Around him the house was silent, the only sound her deep, regular breathing.

Bonnie Baker. She was some piece of work. He'd known it the moment she'd flashed her baby blues at him and tried to get out of that well-deserved speeding ticket.

In the two weeks he'd been staying with Carolyn and Beau, he'd heard stories about Bonnie's various hijinks. He knew she'd been an unruly child who'd dealt her family fits, a rebellious teenager who'd been kicked out of several expensive boarding schools, and now, at the age of twenty-five, she didn't appear to be in any hurry to change her ways. The woman had run out in the middle of her own wedding ceremony, for crying out loud.

Although he didn't know Bonnie Baker for more than the brief time he'd spent with her the night before, he knew enough to make the assessment that she was a young woman who'd had far too much handed to her on a silver platter and believed rules were for others. The kind of woman he needed in his life like an officer of the law needed an old, rusty gun.

He leaned back in the chair and sipped his coffee, his gaze lingering on her. Despite the fact that he disapproved of her life-style and knew she was a spoiled brat, he couldn't help but enjoy her attractiveness.

When Russ had first met Carolyn, he'd thought she was one of the prettiest women ever. But when he'd seen Bonnie, he'd realized Carolyn had merely been a practice model, and the beauty had been perfected with her younger sister.

At the moment most of Bonnie's features were hidden by the pillow she hugged against her face and the tangled spill of her dark hair. Still, those features were fresh in his mind. Bright-blue eyes in a heart-shaped face, a Cupid's-bow mouth that held just a touch of naughtiness. Each and every physical attribute enhanced her overall appeal.

When Carolyn and the twins had left a little while ago to go to the store, she had told him that Bonnie slept like the dead and rarely got up before noon. Russ had immediately envisioned crashing a pair of cymbals over her sleeping head. Something about Ms. Bonnie Baker made him feel perverse.

He sat up straighter in the chair as a moan escaped her. Ah, the beast awakens. She rolled over onto her side, facing him. Her eyelids fluttered, then remained open, widening at the sight of him.

"What are you doing?" she asked, eyes immediately narrowing.

"I'm drinking coffee."

"How long have you been sitting there?"

He smiled thinly, irritated that she could look so alluring first thing in the morning. "Long enough to know you don't snore or drool in your sleep."

"What do you care? You're certainly never going to sleep with me."

She sat up, clutching the sheet against her chest, one of the pink silk spaghetti straps of her nightgown slipping off her smooth shoulder. She shoved her dark hair away from her face and glared at him.

"It's very rude to watch somebody while she sleeps."

"It would be rude if I went into your bedroom and watched you, but your bed is in the middle of the living room."

"And whose fault is that? You could have offered me the bedroom."

Russ grinned and shook his head. "I have a feeling, Princess, that half your problem is that people always give in to you."

"Thank you, Dr. Freud." She got out of the bed with the sheet wrapped around her. "It must be nice to think you have all the answers. Maybe someday I'll be as wise and judgmental as you." With a flourish, she stomped out of the living room and disappeared down the hallway.

Russ's smile faltered. He certainly didn't have all the answers. In fact, most of the time he felt hopelessly out of his depth, floundering in the daily game of survival. Maybe he'd believed he had all the answers at one time, before Anne had walked out on him and Daniel. But when she walked out of their marriage, walked away from him and their son, she'd taken all the answers with her, leaving behind only confusion and chaos.

He drained his coffee cup and stood up, irritated that Bonnie's words had reminded him of just how messed up his life was. He checked his watch. He had an appointment with a Realtor in an hour to look at a house for rent. He was anxious to get settled into his own place and send for Daniel.

Life was much slower paced here in Casey's Corners, and Russ hoped he and his son could heal some of the scars Anne had left.

By the time Russ had rinsed out his coffee cup and placed it in the sink to dry, Bonnie appeared in the kitchen doorway. "Where is everyone else?" she asked, her gaze lingering longingly at the pot of coffee.

"Beau is at work, and Carolyn took the kids to the grocery store." He opened a cabinet door, retrieved a clean mug, then held it out to her.

As she took it, he caught a whiff of her perfume, a spicy fragrance that reminded him instantly of a summer he'd spent in the Orient as a private in the army. The scent was exotically sensual, laden with mystery, and it stirred a flicker of a sexual response deep inside him.

He watched as she poured her coffee, noting how the shorts she wore hugged her shapely derriere and exposed sinful lengths of tanned legs. He wondered if she was that delicious bronze color all over. Weren't most of those European beaches nude beaches?

He frowned, irritated with himself at his thoughts. The last thing he needed to be thinking about was Bonnie Baker's naked, perfumed body. He didn't know her and was sure that if he spent any length of time around her, he wouldn't like her very much.

"So why aren't you at work?" Bonnie asked.

"I work the two-to-ten shift."

"Hmm, I'll remember that and do my speeding before two or after ten." She grinned, a smile filled with playful naughtiness.

"Judging by the collection of tickets I saw in your car last night, I'd imagine your driving days will soon be over. You'll either get your license pulled or find yourself wrapped around a tree." He watched as she sat down at the table and took a sip of her coffee. "You know, I've never understood people like you." He eyed her boldly, his gaze sweeping her face, then continuing down the length of her body in silent assessment.

She didn't flinch beneath his scrutiny, just gazed back at him as one dark eyebrow rose arrogantly. "People like me?"

He nodded. "People who get angry because other people do their jobs. I'm a cop. It's part of my job to give speeders tickets. You were speeding."

"It wasn't the fact that you gave me a ticket that made me mad. It was that you seemed to take such pleasure in it, as if you enjoyed sitting in judgment of me," she said. She looked at him dispassionately. "Tell me something, Russ. Do you wear boxers or briefs?"

"Pardon me?" He felt the blush that started at the base of his neck bring warmth to the tips of his ears. Surely he'd heard her wrong.

"You see, I have this theory. Men who wear briefs are your garden-variety uptight conservatives. Men who play by the rules, never take risks and have little sense of humor. They are judgmental, restrained and controlling."

She paused a moment to sip her coffee, her eyes a darker hue than moments before. "I'm sure my father was a briefs man."

Russ thought he saw a fleeting pain, a hint of vulnerability in the depths of her eyes. It was there only an instant, then gone as she continued.

"I figure it has something to do with briefs cutting off the flow of blood to the brain."

Suddenly Russ wished desperately that beneath his stiff, perfectly creased uniform slacks was a pair of paisley silk boxers. Instead he could almost feel the bands of his briefs constricting, slowly strangling the flow of his blood. "You're crazy," he scoffed.

She grinned triumphantly. "You're definitely a briefs man, Russ."

They both turned as they heard the front door open and close. Carolyn appeared in the kitchen doorway, a toddler riding each hip.

"Oh, my." Bonnie jumped up and reached to take one of the kids. "They are doll babies!" she exclaimed.

Carolyn smiled ruefully. "They were terrors in the grocery store. Brent has learned to get out of the cart, and every time I turned around he was climbing out, and Trent was screaming."

"Which one do I have?" Bonnie asked, cuddling the little boy close to her.

"The escape artist, Brent." Carolyn sank down in a chair and released her hold on Trent, who immediately crawled over to Bonnie and pulled himself up against her leg.

Bonnie grinned with delight. "They like me," she declared.

There was such a look of wonderment, such joy on her face, as if she found the fact that anyone could like her unbelievable. An undefined emotion unfurled in Russ as he watched her sit down. The twins clamored for her attention, crawling on her lap and chattering like monkeys. Russ had always believed that dogs and children had an innate ability to sense a person's true character, no matter how hard that person tried to hide it. He never trusted anyone dogs and children didn't like.

It bothered him that the twins embraced Bonnie so enthusiastically, as if they saw something good in her he had yet to see. He narrowed his eyes, listening as she baby-talked to the boys. Brent managed to crawl up in her lap and grab a handful of her hair. She threw back her head and laughed, a deep, throaty sound that shocked Russ as it sent a wave of pleasure through him. It was the kind of laughter that invited company, and the fact that he wanted to join in irritated him.

The little traitors, he thought. In the past two weeks he'd become close to the twins, yet now they were totally engrossed with Bonnie.

"You have grocery bags in the car?" he asked Carolyn.

She nodded. "I'll get them for you."

He walked out of the house and took a deep breath of the fresh summer air, grateful that it carried no hint of Bonnie's perfume. He'd obviously been on his own too long. It had been fourteen months since Anne had left him, and since that time he hadn't felt a flicker of interest in another woman. But something about Bonnie Baker had reawakened his libido, and he didn't like it one single bit.

When he allowed himself to get interested in a woman again, it would not be an irresponsible, spoiled rich girl like Bonnie Baker. He needed a woman who would be a loving, caring mother for Daniel, a stable woman who understood the needs of children. Because at the moment, Daniel was a bundle of need.

He grabbed the bags of groceries out of Carolyn's car and carried them back into the kitchen. Bonnie was standing on her head against the cabinets, and the twins clapped and giggled with glee. The bottom of her T-shirt had fallen down, exposing an expanse of smooth, tanned stomach.

"Where did Carolyn go?" he asked, averting his gaze.

"She spilled juice on her blouse and went to change." As Russ set the bags on the table, Bonnie pulled her legs down and stood up, her face a becoming pink from the physical exertion. "This is great. They laugh at everything I do."

"Yeah, kids can be pretty accepting," Russ agreed.

"That's what's wonderful about kids, right, fellas?" She leaned down and tousled their fine, blond hair. Then she straightened up and gazed at Russ. "Utter acceptance—you only get it from babies and dogs. I understand you have a son."

Russ nodded. "Daniel. He's eight years old." He felt a sudden ache in his heart for the little boy he'd left in Chicago until he could get settled here.

He was suddenly eager to meet the Realtor, hopeful that the house she would show him would be their new home. It was time for Daniel and him to get on with their lives. He missed his son desperately. He looked at his watch again. "I've got to get out of here. I have an appointment to look at a house for rent."

She grinned at him. "I can't tell you how much I hope you like what you see."

"Yeah, it will be great to get settled in and get Daniel up here."

"Oh, I wasn't thinking about that. I was thinking how nice it would be to have you out of here so I can have that bedroom." She smiled impishly.

He grinned back at her. "Princess, I've got half a mind to reject everything I'm shown and stay here just to keep you sleeping on the sofa—unless, of course, you decide to join me and share the bed." His grin widened. "Who knows, you might just discover that during the day I'm a briefs man, but at night I turn into a wild, crazy, boxers kind of guy."

She stared at him in surprise, then threw back her head and laughed, once again the sound of it shooting warmth through him. The twins laughed with her, clapping in excitement. "Perhaps in your dreams," she finally answered, sobering only slightly when Carolyn walked back into the kitchen.

"What's so funny?" Carolyn asked, looking first at Russ, then at Bonnie.

"Absolutely nothing," Russ replied stiffly. "I've got an appointment. See you tonight." Without waiting for a reply, he left the room, and a moment later the front door slammed with more force than necessary.

Carolyn gazed at Bonnie reproachfully. "What did you do to him?"

"Nothing!" Bonnie sank down in a chair, as a frown creased her forehead. "He hates me."

"Don't be ridiculous," Carolyn scoffed as she began putting away the groceries. "He doesn't even know you."

"What he knows about me he hates, and I don't blame him one bit." She sighed, discouragement sweeping through her. She'd always had a disconcerting knack for pushing people away from her, saying and doing things to make them back off. "Since the moment I met him last night, I've gone out of my way to be outrageous. I just can't seem to help myself. Of course, I don't care what he thinks about me," she said with a touch of bravado, then continued more softly, "sometimes I just confuse myself."

Carolyn grinned. "Honey, you've confused me since the moment you were born twenty-five years ago." She got a plastic bowl filled with blocks out of a lower cabinet and set it on the floor for the boys.

Bonnie watched the children, embracing their laughter to her heart. There hadn't been much laughter in the Baker house when she was growing up. "I envy you, Carolyn," she said softly. "Someday I'd like to have what you've found here."

Carolyn sat down at the table across from her and grabbed her hands. "Bonnie, I want these things for you, too. I thought maybe you'd found them with that prince you were supposed to marry."

Bonnie shook her head, remembering how close she had come to ruining her life. "Helmut was a great guy and a lot of fun. I got caught up in the parties and the prewedding excitement. I wanted so badly to be in love, but I wasn't. It wasn't until I was about to walk down the aisle that I realized marriage to Helmut wasn't what I wanted. He expected me to be the party girl, so for a while that's what I was, but that's not me." She grinned. "Unfortunately, I'm not sure who *me* is."

Carolyn nodded. "I didn't discover who I was and exactly what I wanted until I came here to gain custody of the twins. Remember I thought I'd fight Beau for custody, then take the kids back to New York and continue my work at the corporation. Falling in love with Beau changed all that.''

Bonnie knew Carolyn had come to Casey's Corners when her best friends had died in a tragic car accident, leaving the twins parentless and their custody up in the air. Carolyn was their godmother and Beau Randolf their godfather, and Bonnie was grateful to everyone that instead of a custody suit, love had decided the issue.

Bonnie looked at the little boys once again, then at her sister. "I always knew you'd be a terrific mother."

Carolyn laughed ruefully. "I have to admit, there are days I worry about it. We didn't exactly have the best role models as parents. Mother and Father were wonderful at making money, but they weren't very good at raising a family."

Bonnie nodded, aware Carolyn was right. None of the Baker girls knew anything about family life. They had had little of it when growing up. Their mother, before her death, had spent her time flying from one lush vacation spot to another. Their father had either been at work in the plastics corporation they owned or en route to some exotic location to open a branch office. The Baker children had been raised by nannies and servants.

What little closeness they'd had with one another had shredded to pieces two months ago when their father had been found murdered in his office and an eyewitness had seen their brother running from the scene. "Has there been any word from Sam?"

Carolyn's face clouded darkly. "Nothing. I just can't understand it. I know he had nothing to do with Father's murder, but I can't understand why he's on the run, why he hasn't contacted any of us."

"I checked all the business associates in Europe to see if any of them have seen or talked to Sam, but nobody has heard from him," Bonnie replied, despair welling up in her throat as she thought of her elder brother. "What about Colleen and Julianne? Have they heard from him at all?" Bonnie asked, referring to the youngest Baker sibling and Sam's wife.

"No, nothing. Sam was here in Casey's Corners a couple of weeks ago. You know he was friends with the twins' parents before the accident. When Beau and I went to their house to pick up some things for the boys, I found Sam's address book in their spare bedroom. We asked all around town, and finally one of the waitresses in the café told us she'd served him coffee. Then he'd walked out to the highway. She'd assumed he was looking to hitch a ride out of town." Carolyn stood up and poured herself a cup of coffee. "It's been a couple of weeks since he walked down that highway, and it's as if the highway swallowed him up."

Bonnie reached up and grabbed the gold phoenix charm that hung around her neck. Her father had given one to each of his children just days before his death. Bonnie was ambivalent about what the charm represented. On one hand, it was precious to her because it was the last thing her father would ever give her. On the other, it was a constant reminder that he was now gone, and she would never again have a chance to win his love.

She got up from the table, disturbed by her thoughts. She didn't want to think about the dysfunction of her family, didn't want to dwell on the aching loss of both her father and her brother. It all hurt too deep, too much.

"I don't suppose there are any good singles night-clubs in town, are there?"

Carolyn laughed. "I've heard the VFW is an action-packed place. The only problem is, most of the singles are over the age of sixty-five."

Bonnie leaned against the sink, watching as Carolyn put away the last of the groceries. "I just wish I'd meet some guy and there would be instant chemistry. You know, he'd look at me, and I'd look at him, and we'd know instantly that we were in love."

Carolyn snorted derisively. "That's the way I always expected it to work, too. But it certainly didn't happen that way with Beau. Do you want some breakfast?"

Bonnie shook her head. "Tell me about you and Beau."

Carolyn sat down at the table, her face animated with happiness. "When I first met Beau, I thought he was the most arrogant, obnoxious man I'd ever met. I couldn't stand him. There was chemistry, all right, but it was all the wrong kind."

"So what happened? How did it change?"

"I don't know." Carolyn held her hands out in a gesture of helplessness. "All I know is at some point I realized I couldn't bear the thought of not having him in my life, of not sharing my dreams, my days and my nights with him." She smiled fondly at Bonnie. "You have to watch this love stuff. It sneaks up on you when you least expect it. If people had told me a year ago I would be married to Beau, I would have told them they were crazy." She grinned and began wiping down the high-chair trays. "Who knows? Perhaps a year from now you and Russ will be married. Crazier things have happened."

"Now it's you who's talking crazy." Bonnie laughed in protest. "There is positively no way. I know the kind of man I want as a husband, and believe me, it's not that uptight, rigid cop with an attitude."

Carolyn moved to the stove, then turned and smiled at Bonnie. "You have the mistaken belief that somehow you can control these things. Believe me, you can't."

"We'll see," Bonnie said with a healthy dose of self-assurance. Carolyn wasn't factoring in one very important part of the equation. Even if, in a moment of insanity, Bonnie found herself attracted to Russ, there was no way he would ever be attracted to her. In the brief time he'd known her, he'd made it perfectly clear he didn't like her.

She remembered the disdain that had darkened his eyes when he'd gazed at her so critically. His eyes were the color of hot cocoa, but there had been no warmth in them. Even his tone of voice held a vague scorn when he spoke to her. No way, no how.

No, there could never be a love match between the two of them. The best they could hope for was that they wouldn't kill each other before Russ found a home of his own and Bonnie got his bedroom.

Chapter Three

Bonnie woke up suddenly. Sam. It was only a dream. He was running down an endless highway, running so hard that sweat gleamed on his skin and his breath came in harsh pants. Every few minutes he turned his head and yelled something back at her, but she couldn't understand him, couldn't discern what he said. She only knew his facial features were twisted with anguish, and he was warning her of danger. Imminent danger. No matter how hard she ran after him, she couldn't catch him, couldn't lessen the distance between them.

Her heart ached in frustration, her need to find him, help him, filled her with a deep, aching anguish. Why, Sam? Why are you running? No matter how bad the circumstances looked surrounding the murder, she knew in her heart that Sam had nothing to do with their father's death. So many questions, and absolutely no answers.

"Ouch!" The yelp was followed by a string of muttered curses, pulling Bonnie out of her horrid dream.

"Wha . . . who's there?" She sat straight up, blinking to focus in the darkness.

Against the faint illumination from the street lamp, seeping in around the edges of the curtains, she made out a shadowy, broad-shouldered figure. "Who's there?" she repeated in alarm.

"It's me. Russ." His voice sounded funny, and with a moan he sank down on the edge of her bed.

"What are you doing? Get off of there." She kicked out her feet, connecting with the solid wall of his back.

"Hey, stop that," he protested, his breath hissing between clenched teeth. "Just let me catch my wind a minute. I think I broke my toe on the bed frame." His shoes clunked to the floor, and he moaned again. "This is what I get for trying to be thoughtful and taking off my shoes to be more quiet."

Bonnie reached over and turned on the light next to the bed, casting the room in a soft light. She rubbed her eyes, attempting to banish the last of the bad dream. The room was stuffy and she was unsure whether the perspiration at her hairline was due to the heat or the intensity of her dream. She drew in a deep breath, then looked at Russ, who massaged his big toe through his sock. "Do you think it's broken?"

"I don't think so. But damn, it hurts." He pulled his shoes back on and stood. "I'm sorry I woke you up. I was trying to sneak in, but I didn't count on stubbing my toe."

"Actually, I'm glad you woke me up. I was having a nightmare."

"Was it the one where you're on a beach and realize you've forgotten your suntan lotion? Or maybe the one where you're in a store and can't find your charge card?"

Bonnie gazed at him scathingly. "You really are something."

He shrugged, although his cheeks flushed slightly. "I call 'em like I see 'em."

"Then you'd better check into a pair of glasses," she returned irritably. She threaded her fingers through her hair, pulling it away from her face. "What time is it anyway?"

"Almost one."

She looked at him in surprise. "I thought you got off duty at ten."

"I do. After work Waylon, the other deputy, and I had a couple of beers." He smiled mockingly. "Of course, had I known you'd be waiting up for me, I would have hurried directly here."

Bonnie snorted, not even dignifying his remark with a reply. Grabbing her robe from the side of the sofa bed, she pulled it on, unwilling to go back to sleep with her dream still so fresh in her mind.

"What are you doing?" he asked as she flung her legs over the side of the bed and stood up.

"Not that it's any of your business, but I'm going to have a glass of milk and a piece of cake."

"Sounds great. Do you mind if I join you?"

"Yes, I do," she answered, knowing he would anyway. She turned on the kitchen light as she entered, intensely aware of his limping presence just behind her. Ignoring him, she got herself a piece of cake and a glass of milk, then put the remainder of the cake and the milk jug back in the refrigerator. She sat down at the table and began to eat.

He chuckled and retrieved the items from the fridge. "So, Princess," he said as he joined her at the table. "How long do you intend to be in town?"

She shrugged and smiled. "I figure as long as I can be the bane of your existence, my mission here isn't complete."

He paused a moment, gazing at her speculatively. "You think we could call a truce for a few minutes?" he asked. "I've had a few beers, I'm feeling pretty mellow and verbal sparring always gives me indigestion."

"You started it by making fun of my nightmare," she reminded him.

He nodded. "You're right. I apologize."

Bonnie eyed him suspiciously, unsure if she should believe him. She decided he looked sincere. "Apology accepted," she finally replied.

"So, what did you all do this evening while I was out risking limb and life to keep this little town safe from criminal activity?" He joined her at the table, sitting across from her.

"Not much. Caro, Beau and I mostly talked, catching up on one another's lives. It's nice to see Caro happy, and Beau seems like a nice guy."

"As far as I'm concerned, he's one of the best," Russ stated. "I couldn't believe it when he offered me the job, then his hospitality here until I got settled in my own place."

Bonnie nodded. After spending the evening with her brother-in-law, she could attest to his charity. She'd finally admitted to Carolyn and Beau that she was broke. Beau had instantly offered her a loan, but she'd declined, instead asking him if he knew of any jobs in town. She'd seen a momentary flicker of respect in his eyes as he promised to keep his ears open for anyone hiring.

Russ interrupted her thoughts. "So, tell me about your nightmare."

She shook her head, unwilling to share her dreams with this man she barely knew and wasn't at all certain she liked. Besides, she wasn't sure she wanted him to know that her brother was a fugitive from justice. "I barely remember it now."

"Hmm, too bad. They say you can tell a lot about people by analyzing their dreams."

"Or sorting through their garbage."

Russ laughed and Bonnie's breath caught in her throat. She'd assumed his laugh would sound strained, uptight, but instead it was robust, filled with life. It disconcerted her. Why was his laugh so...so pleasant? She focused on the piece of chocolate cake in front of her for a moment, suddenly aware that the kitchen seemed too small and far too warm. "Why is it so hot in here?"

"It's August. The dog days of summer."

"Don't Carolyn and Beau have an air-conditioner?"

"No, they don't." He grinned at her look of disbelief. "Part of small-town charm. People from Kansas come from hardy stock. A little heat doesn't bother them."

She eyed him curiously. "Carolyn told me you're from Chicago. Being an officer out here in Casey's Corners must be quite a bit different."

Before answering, he popped a bite of his cake into his mouth, then washed it down with a gulp of milk. "All the difference in the world. Police work in a big city is much more intense. It leaves time for little else in your life."

"Is that why your wife left you?" Bonnie instantly bit her lip, feeling bad the question had slipped out. "Sorry, that's none of my business."

"It's all right. It's no big secret. Yes and no, my work certainly contributed to Anne leaving. But we'd had problems from the very beginning of our marriage. Anne was young when we married, and Daniel came along right away." He leaned back in the chair and frowned as if he regretted saying so much. "In any case, Daniel and I are looking forward to a fresh start here."

A fresh start. That sounded wonderful. That's what she wanted, also. A fresh start to work at happiness, to build something lasting. She wanted to shove away all the unhappiness of the past once and for all.

As Russ continued to concentrate on eating his cake, Bonnie focused on him, noting the faint shadow of whisker growth that darkened his chin and emphasized the lean planes of his cheeks. The cleft in his chin was provocative, offsetting the strength and boldness of his other features. There was no getting around it— the man was something of a hunk.

Whatever he had drunk in the bar before coming home had apparently relaxed him. He appeared more at ease, his face not as strained. She was startled to realize they were actually having a civil conversation. She wondered if it would be possible to keep him pleasantly buzzed for the remainder of the time they shared their living space.

"Do I have frosting on my nose or something?" he asked, a grin tugging at one corner of his mouth, letting her know he was aware of her scrutiny.

"Or something," she answered as warmth crept into her cheeks.

He laughed, as if enjoying the fact that he'd caused her to blush. "Don't worry, Princess. You won't have to put up with me anymore after tonight."

She looked at him in surprise. "The house you saw today?"

"Is perfect and I'm moving out first thing in the morning and sending for Daniel tomorrow afternoon."

"Well, that's wonderful." For a moment Bonnie was shocked by the swift wave of disappointment that washed through her. She realized a little piece of her enjoyed tormenting the handsome cop and would miss the daily opportunity to do so. "Tell me about the house."

He shrugged. "It's a lot like this one. Three bedrooms, a huge tree in the backyard, perfect for climbing. It needs a little work, but it's a rental with an option to buy. First thing in the morning I'll get my furniture out of storage, and before you know it, the place will be home."

Home. Bonnie's heart fluttered with a wistful longing. The huge mansion she had been raised in had never been a home. A museum of fine things, the status-symbol residence of a successful man and his family—but there had been no warmth, no sense of home.

She got up and took her plate and glass to the sink, unwilling to dwell on thoughts of the past any longer. It was time for her to look ahead, to the future.

Russ joined her at the sink with his dirty dishes. He thrust a dish towel into her hand. "I'll wash, you dry. We don't want to leave the dirty dishes for Carolyn to face in the morning." He turned on the faucet, then raised an eyebrow sardonically. "You do know how to dry dishes, don't you?"

"Of course. I know how to do a lot of things," Bonnie snapped. Old emotions rolled to the surface. She hated feeling inadequate, and his question implied her worthlessness. She'd spent most of her childhood hearing about her worthlessness. She'd be damned if she'd listen to it now.

She grabbed the glass he held out to her and jammed the towel and her hand inside. She swished the towel around, then attempted to pull her hand out. Stuck. The towel had somehow wrapped itself around her wrist; her hand wouldn't fit through the glass opening.

Trying again, she turned away from Russ so he couldn't see she had a slight problem. This is ridiculous, she thought, trying unsuccessfully to get the glass off.

A burst of half-hysterical laughter rose to her lips as she imagined going through the rest of her life with a glass on her hand. Swallowing the laugh before it could escape, she tugged on the glass once again. No luck.

"What's the matter?" Russ asked, holding out the other glass to her.

"Nothing," she answered quickly. She'd rather go through life wearing a glass than ask him for help. Then, realizing she couldn't do that, she turned and faced him. "If you laugh I swear you'll be sorry." She held up her glass-encased hand. "It's stuck."

He fought his laugh, his lips compressed tightly, but his eyes danced in merriment as he shook his head. "You are some piece of work, Princess."

"Don't call me that," she protested as he took her hand in his. She was mortified, humiliated by the whole thing.

"Just hold still," he commanded. As he gently twisted the glass, Bonnie couldn't help but notice he had nice hands. Big, capable ones, with slender fingers that radiated warmth.

He stood so close to her she could smell the evocative scent of his cologne, the musky odor mingling with the more subtle scent of soap and the lingering remnant of beer. It was a distinctly masculine smell that caused a sweet heat to rush through her.

She was also uncomfortably aware of his body, intimately close to hers. Dark chest hairs peeked out over the unbuttoned portion of his shirt and she wondered how they would feel against her cheek. Would they be scratchy and stiff or soft and feathery? She fought the impulse to lean her face into him and find out.

Cooler night air drifted in through the open window above the sink, pleasant against her heated skin and adding to the sensory enjoyment of the moment.

"There," he said softly as the glass finally popped off her hand. For a moment they remained unmoving, his fingers still wrapped warmly around her wrist. He raised his gaze to her face, and in his eyes she saw a flame of fire, a flicker of desire. Her knees weakened, making it impossible for her to move away. He wanted to kiss her—she could see it in his eyes. And she wanted him to, wanted desperately.

His face moved closer to hers, his mouth only inches away. Without thought, she parted her lips expectantly. For a moment his gaze burned into hers, his breath sweet and warm as it fanned her face. He grinned down at her and drew back. "I told you before, Princess. I suspect half your problem is that you always get what you want, and you want to be kissed way too badly for me to comply."

It took a moment for his words to sink in, but as they did, she stumbled back from him, jerking her wrist out of his grip. "You...you thought I wanted you to kiss me? Don't be ridiculous," she said with as much indignation as she could muster. "If you'd tried, I would have bitten off your lower lip." She slapped the dish towel down on the counter. "And just for that, you can finish the dishes by yourself." Without waiting for his reply, she turned and stomped out of the kitchen.

Russ breathed a sigh of relief when she'd gone. That had been close. Too close. For just a moment, he'd almost fallen into a state of total insanity. As she'd stood next to him, her hair tousled and her scent surrounding him, he'd nearly given in to his desire to kiss her, mold her body against his own, touch that tanned, smooth flesh that seemed to exist only to tease him.

He didn't like it. Didn't like it one bit. Bonnie Baker managed to affect him in a decidedly adverse way. Frowning, he remembered taunting her to share the bedroom the night before, challenging her to discover if he was a wild boxers man after dark. It had been out of line, uncharacteristic, and what was worse, he found himself almost wishing she'd taken him up on it.

He finished the last of the dishes, then splashed water on his forehead. What he really needed was a cold shower. He'd been alone too long, was achingly vulnerable to Bonnie's sweet curves, the fire in her eyes. Of course, he would be vulnerable to any sexually attractive woman. He was a healthy thirty-year-old man who'd spent the past year like a monk.

He grinned and shook his head ruefully. The last thing he needed was to get involved with an irresponsible, flighty, mouthy woman like Bonnie Baker. He was glad he hadn't kissed her. He had a feeling he would like kissing her...would like it a lot. There was no point in messing up a perfectly good case of healthy animosity with something as fleeting as sexual desire.

He needed to stay focused on Daniel, not on a woman who would probably not last here in Casey's Corners a full week. He wasn't the type to indulge in brief affairs, and that's all he would want from Bonnie. A brief, uncomplicated, completely sexual relationship.

He was ready to find a woman who would become his wife. He knew what kind of woman he and Daniel needed, and it was definitely not Bonnie Baker. She'd run out on her wedding to a prince: she certainly wasn't the kind of woman he'd choose to be his life partner, his helpmate and the stepmother to his son. He needed a woman who understood children, whose sole commitment was to the family, not the latest fashions. And Bonnie certainly wouldn't want the kind of life he lived. She was probably accustomed to exquisite dining in exotic restaurants or hopping on a jet for a day of shopping.

He sank back down at the table, for a moment his mind filled with a vision of his son. Things had been difficult since Anne had left them. Russ had coped with the failed marriage by throwing himself into his job, easing his anger and sense of betrayal by long hours of police work. Daniel was the one who had suffered, first from his mother's abandonment, then by Russ's absence. Before Russ knew it, his loving, sweet son was out of control.

He rubbed his eyes, envisioning Daniel's dark brown eyes and stubborn chin. All too often those eyes had been filled with rage and that little chin had lifted defiantly. Russ rubbed his eyes once again, hoping that here in the smaller town, with more time to spend with Daniel, he could find the key to healing the little boy's hurt.

Things will be better here, Russ thought optimistically. He intended to give his son plenty of attention and gentle understanding. Casey's Corners was just what they needed, but Bonnie Baker certainly wasn't.

It was a good thing he was moving out tomorrow. His body obviously didn't understand his brain's desire to steer clear of Bonnie. He grinned again as he thought of her hand stuck in the glass. He was sure she would rather have worn that glass for the rest of her life than ask his help in extracting her hand.

He neatly folded the dish towel and set it on the counter, then shut off the light and went back through the living room. As he walked by the sofa bed, Bonnie rolled over.

"Kiss you? Huh, I'd rather kiss a toad." Her voice was soft but firm.

Russ chuckled and went into the bedroom. Yes, she was some piece of work.

Chapter Four

"Nervous?" Beau asked Bonnie as they walked together down the sidewalk toward Main Street. It was Monday and the early-morning sun was already hot on their backs.

Bonnie hesitated a moment, then nodded. "I hate to admit it, but I am. I've never had a real job before. There was a time I thought I wanted to work in the family business, but when I broached my father about it, he laughed." She knew she was talking too much. When she was nervous she always ran on at the mouth. "Of course, Sam and Caro both worked for the corporation. They were the brains in the family. I've always been the party girl."

"It takes a lot of brains to know when it's time to quit partying and get down to life," Beau observed. Bonnie shot him a grateful smile.

"You did say you could type, right?"

"Of course." She didn't quite meet his gaze, hoping she'd be forgiven for this little white lie. "But you said there wouldn't be a lot of typing," she reminded him.

He nodded. "Mostly we need somebody to answer the phone and take information. Occasionally reports have to be typed, but not too often." He smiled reassuringly. "Don't worry, we're a small-town police station. Things are fairly laid-back. You'll do fine."

Bonnie hoped so. She knew Beau was giving her a chance, putting her to work at the station. When he'd mentioned the possibility the night before, her instinct had been to decline. He'd told her they needed some temporary help because they were finally going to a computer system.

It was Caro who'd finally convinced her to give it a try. "You'll be working with Brenda Jo, and she's a real doll. Besides, it's only temporary. It will be good training." Caro had finally convinced Bonnie to take the job.

She couldn't wait to see Russ's face when he walked in this afternoon and realized she was working there.

True to his word, Russ had gotten up early Saturday morning, and by noon had all his things packed and out of Caro and Beau's place. Bonnie had moved into the bedroom, and that night, lying in the double bed, she'd been surrounded by Russ's scent. It lingered in the air, clung to the mattress despite the clean sheets beneath her. She remembered that moment they had shared in the kitchen, when his lips had been so achingly close to hers. He had been right. She'd wanted him to kiss her, and that knowledge irritated the hell out of her. She'd slept poorly, aggravated by the thought that the man could torment her despite his absence.

"Russ won't be happy about me working at the station." She spoke her thoughts aloud.

Beau shrugged. "Russ isn't the boss. I am."

"He really dislikes me. He thinks I'm worthless and irresponsible, selfish and shallow."

Beau raised an eyebrow. "He told you that?"

"He didn't have to. I see it in his expressions whenever he looks at me or talks to me."

"Maybe he'll change his mind. He doesn't know you very well yet."

She grinned gamely. "It doesn't matter. I've spent my whole life not caring what other people think. Besides, I don't intend to give him a chance to know me any better." She straightened her shoulders and raised her chin. "I don't have to prove myself to anyone...especially not some small-town cop. I am what I am, and people either accept me or they don't."

Beau merely smiled. "And what are you?"

Bonnie hesitated a moment, the question rolling around in her head without a solid answer. She finally looked up at Beau. "I'm a party girl who presently finds herself without party funds. A temporary setback that will change soon, then I'll be off again visiting royalty, drinking champagne and indulging myself in an extravagant lifestyle." The words sounded ridiculously frivolous and caused an ache deep in her heart. She shoved away the pain and smiled brightly at Beau. "Every family has a black sheep. And in mine, I'm it."

"I'd say Sam is running neck in neck with you for that particular title," Beau answered.

Bonnie frowned, suddenly remembering the dream of Sam running down a highway, scared and alone, that had haunted her the past several nights. Her heart ached with Sam's ominous absence from them all. "Sam isn't a black sheep. He's one of the good guys. He's just gotten himself caught up in something bad."

"That's what Carolyn keeps telling me. But the evidence doesn't look good."

"You mean because a witness saw Sam running away from the office where Father was shot?"

Beau nodded. "That combined with the fact that he hasn't turned himself in to the police. Apparently your father and Sam had a heated fight right before the murder."

Bonnie laughed. "Every argument with my father turned into a heated fight." She sobered slightly. "My father was not an easy man to get along with, and he and Sam constantly butted heads. That certainly doesn't mean Sam killed him."

Beau smiled at her. "You and your sister think alike. I'll say this for you—you Baker sisters are loyal when it comes to your brother and sisters."

"They're all I have in my life." They turned onto Main Street and all thoughts of Sam flew from Bonnie's head as they approached the small, brick building that housed the police department.

Her first job. Nerves jangled inside her like tiny electrical shorts. The burden of Beau's trust weighed heavily. What if she messed up? What if she did something horrible? Please don't let me screw this up, she thought desperately.

As they walked into the office, the woman at the front desk greeted Beau.

"Hey, boss."

She stood up and Bonnie realized she must be almost six feet tall. Big boned, with carrot-red hair, she eyed Bonnie with open curiosity.

"Hi, Brenda Jo. I brought you some help," Beau replied.

"Hallelujah. I've been overworked and underpaid for years."

Beau grinned. "I can't do anything about the underpaid part, but Bonnie is here to lessen your work load." He turned to Bonnie and made quick, formal introductions. "You'll be working directly under

Brenda Jo. And don't let her fool you, Bonnie. She's the real boss around here. She keeps us all on our toes."

Brenda Jo laughed and shoved her red hair away from her broad face. "I have to be tough to put up with all the testosterone in this building." She stood up and placed a hand on Bonnie's arm. "Come on, sweetheart, I'll show you around. It will be good to have another female in this joint."

For the next fifteen minutes Brenda Jo gave Bonnie a tour of the building. "As you can see, we're a pretty small operation," she explained. "Thankfully serious crime hasn't found us here in Casey's Corners yet."

Bonnie peeked into one of the two holding cells and shivered slightly. "I spent a miserable night in a cell much like this in Paris."

Brenda Jo stared at her in shock. "Don't tell me Beau went and hired me a jailbird?"

Bonnie suddenly realized she should have kept her mouth shut. "It was nothing serious," she said hurriedly. "A bunch of us were arrested for disturbing the peace. We'd had a little too much champagne and decided to swim in one of the fountains. We all found it very amusing. Unfortunately the Paris officials didn't."

Brenda Jo laughed. "Oh, well, that I can understand. Old man Milford Jones gets his nose in the sauce about twice a year and tries to climb the water tower. We haul him in and hold him until he sobers up." She eyed Bonnie curiously once again. "You've been to Paris, huh? I've always wanted to go there."

"So, why don't you?" Bonnie asked.

Brenda Jo laughed. "Honey, I'm almost fifty years old and have never been out of Kansas." For a moment her hazel eyes were hazy and a soft smile curved her lips. "Everyone needs a dream. Paris in the springtime just happens to be mine. The Champs-Élysées and the Arc de Triomphe, the Seine River and the Tuileries Gardens."

"For somebody who's not been there, you know a lot about it."

Brenda Jo grinned. "Travel books. I read them for fun. Come on, I'll finish the grand tour."

Fifteen minutes later, as Bonnie filed a stack of folders Brenda Jo had given her, she thought of the older woman's words. Everyone needed a dream. How many years had it been since Bonnie had had a dream for herself?

When she was little, she'd dreamed her family was broke. She'd dreamed of a father who worked nine to five, and a mother who baked cookies from scratch and never went away. She'd watched corny movies where the family was poor but their hovel was filled with love, and she envied those people, wanted that for herself.

By the time she was ten, she'd put away her childish dreams, and there had been no others to take their place. "Dreams are for kids," she muttered. If you had no dreams or expectations, then you were never disappointed. And nobody else could be disappointed in you.

"Here, hon, when you finish that filing, these reports need to be typed." Brenda Jo handed her a bulging manila envelope. "When you're ready, the typewriter is on the desk in the storage room. Not the best environment, but it's quiet back there."

"Uh, Beau said there wouldn't be much typing," Bonnie hedged.

Brenda Jo grinned. "I never tell the sheriff how backed up I am. Is there a problem?"

"No, it's just that I'm not a very fast typist," Bonnie explained.

"Don't worry about that," Brenda Jo assured her. "Some of those have been sitting here for a month or two. It won't matter if it takes a couple of hours to get them all done."

A couple of hours? Bonnie felt the bulky folder and her heart sank. She would be lucky to have all these typed up in a couple of months.

After finishing the filing, Bonnie went back into the storage room. Seating herself at the desk, she stared at the typewriter in front of her. The information on the forms was handwritten and all she had to do was type it onto another form. "Piece of cake," she muttered, rolling one of the forms into the typewriter.

It was several hours later when Bonnie took a break, pausing a moment to rub first her eyes, then the back of her neck. The trash basket next to the desk was filled with forms she'd mistyped, but she had ten perfect ones in a new folder. At this rate, it wouldn't take months to complete the work, but it would take weeks.

She rolled a new form into the typewriter and began her hunt-and-peck work.

"You weren't kidding when you said you typed slow."

Bonnie looked up sheepishly at the sound of Brenda Jo's voice.

"As I said, Beau told me there wouldn't be very much typing. I figured I could fake it." Bonnie stood up, heart heavy as she reached for her purse. A couple of hours on the job and she was about to be fired.

Brenda Jo grinned. "Hell, I've faked worse things than my typing skills. I just came in to tell you it's past time for your lunch break. You get an hour." She glanced at her watch. "It's one-thirty now. Be back by two-thirty."

"You mean I'm not fired?" Bonnie looked at her incredulously.

"Nah. Who else could I hire in this one-horse town who can tell me about Paris? Now, go get some lunch and be back on time."

Bonnie hardly wasted a moment leaving the police station. Once on the sidewalk, she hesitated, unsure what to do about food. With an hour to spare, she could walk back to Caro's and eat there, but the sun was warm, the day too gorgeous to spend cooped up in a house. Instead she opted for buying a sandwich at the nearby café and eating it on the park bench in front of the station.

Minutes later, armed with a tuna-salad sandwich, chips and a soda, Bonnie relaxed on the bench and ate her lunch while watching the afternoon shoppers drifting in and out of the stores.

She had to admit, Casey's Corners had a certain charm. Trees lined the street, lending welcome shade to the sidewalks. The pace was slower, and people took time to stop and visit before going on their way. Caro's letters had been filled with praise for the little town she now called home. She'd written about the warmth of the people, the feeling of belonging she'd gained in living here. Someday Bonnie wanted to feel that sense of belonging.

Finishing her lunch, she gathered her trash and disposed of it in a receptacle close by. She checked her watch, then sat back down, realizing she had a good thirty minutes before she had to be back at work.

She sat up straighter as she saw Russ in the distance, walking toward her. The sunshine played on his dark hair, making the auburn highlights look fiery. She couldn't help but notice how fine he appeared in his uniform, his shoulders straight with pride and his strides long and self-assured. Drat the man anyway, she thought, unsure what exactly it was about him that so irritated her.

She knew the moment he saw her. His eyes widened, then a lazy smirk of amusement lifted the corners of his mouth and deepened the cleft in his chin.

"Come to pay those speeding tickets, Princess?"

"Must you call me that?"

He shrugged and sank down on the bench next to her. "Consider it my pet name for you."

Bonnie frowned. Most pet names were said affectionately, but when Russ called her 'Princess,' it always sounded sarcastic and uncomplimentary. "So, what are you doing here?" he asked curiously.

She smiled. "I'm on my lunch break."

The pupils of his eyes flared in surprise. "You have a job?"

"Started this morning."

"Where? At the café?" he asked.

She shook her head.

"At the drugstore?"

Again she shook her head.

"You might say we're co-workers." She grinned impishly at his look of disbelief.

"You're kidding. What kind of work are you doing?"

"Filing, answering phones, typing." She waved her hands airily. "The usual office kind of work."

"You know how to type?"

His look of utter disbelief only fed her irritation. "Of course I know how to type." She raised an eyebrow arrogantly. "I might have been born with a silver spoon in my mouth, but I had to learn to polish it myself."

Russ stared at her for a long moment, then laughed. Again Bonnie felt warmth flare in the pit of her stomach at the pleasant sound of his laughter. Why did he have the kind of laughter that made her want to join in? And why did it always seem to be at her expense?

"I guess you got all settled into the new place?" she asked.

"Yeah. It's great. You'll have to come over, see the place and meet Daniel."

This time it was her turn to look at him in surprise. "I... I'd like that," she said, confused because it was true.

"Oops, I've got to get inside. I'm already late." He stood up and eyed her expectantly. "You coming?"

She shook her head. "I still have fifteen minutes of my lunch hour left. I'll just sit here and enjoy the sunshine." She closed her eyes and leaned her head back against the building.

Russ stared at her for a long moment, then turned and went inside, her sun-kissed vision still painted in his mind. Damn, what had ever possessed him to invite her to his home? And why on earth would he want her to meet Daniel?

"Hey, Brenda Jo," he greeted as he walked in the door. "I hear Beau finally hired you some help."

Brenda Jo nodded. "Bonnie. Gonna be nice to have another female around here."

Russ sat down at his desk across the room and grinned. "Well, if I were you, I wouldn't get too used to having her around."

"Why is that?"

"From what I've heard about Bonnie Baker, she'll get bored pretty quickly and move on. She's not a long-haul kind of woman."

Brenda Jo shrugged. "Then I guess I'll just enjoy her company while she's here." Brenda Jo grinned. "Did you know she got arrested in Paris for swimming in a fountain?"

An instant vision of Bonnie naked and frolicking in a fountain exploded in Russ's mind. Sparkling drops of water clung to her bronzed skin, taunting him, tormenting him. He shook his head to dislodge the vision. "Nothing Bonnie Baker has done would surprise me," he finally said.

Their conversation was interrupted by a phone call—a report of a break-in at a farmhouse ten miles out of town. Russ grabbed the patrol car keys and started out the door, bumping into Bonnie as she came inside.

"Off to arrest unsuspecting speeders?" she asked.

Russ scowled, refusing to feel guilty about ticketing her. "I'd better not ever have to arrest you for skinny-dipping in a fountain in this town."

Her eyes widened in surprise, then she grinned, that slightly naughty, impish smile that caused his blood to heat.

"Okay, I promise not to go skinny-dipping in any fountains." Her smile deepened. "But I can't make that same promise about local ponds."

Russ felt his scowl increase as Brenda Jo laughed, and again an image of a wet, naked Bonnie erupted in his brain. "I've got to go. I've got work to do."

"Go get 'em, Dirty Harry," Bonnie said.

With the scowl still biting his forehead, he left the building. He got in the car, started the engine and turned the air conditioning on high, waiting a moment for the blowing air to cool.

Physical attraction, that's all it is, he assured himself. There was no denying Bonnie was sexually magnetic. But he had absolutely no desire to get involved with her. He shook his head with a smile. Unless involvement consisted of a couple of hours beneath a sheet.

He put the car in gear and pulled away from the curb, his thoughts still on the physical delights of Bonnie. Unfortunately, when he'd found himself a single father he'd sworn to himself there wouldn't be a parade of women through his life and Daniel's.

Despite his attraction to Ms. Baker, he knew she was not the kind of woman he'd want to marry and so there was no way he'd follow through on it. He wanted a wife, somebody he could share his life with, somebody who would be a partner in raising Daniel. He didn't need a short-term lust affair.

Daniel. He tightened his grip on the steering wheel as his thoughts turned to his son. Since arriving on Saturday, Daniel had been sullen, and Russ was at a loss on how to break through the child's moodiness. One minute he was angry and filled with rage; the next he was in tears.

Damn Anne and her need for freedom. It was forgivable that she hadn't wanted to be married to him any longer. It was unforgivable that she no longer wanted to parent their child. He had a feeling his ex-wife and Bonnie had a lot in common. Although Anne had not been wealthy, she'd been spoiled by doting parents. Whenever trouble had cropped up in their marriage, she'd run home. It had always been easier for her to flee than to stick around and solve problems. Russ had a feeling Bonnie was the same. When things got tough and weren't fun anymore, she'd hop on a plane and fly off to another area to play. Definitely not long-term-relationship material, and Russ wasn't interested in anything but long-term. When it came to women, he was definitely a traditional, uptight, briefs kind of guy. He knew exactly what he wanted in a wife, and Bonnie Baker wasn't it.

As he pulled up in front of the farmhouse, he shoved away all personal thoughts, mentally readying himself for the police work ahead.

It was after eleven that night when Russ finally got back to the station. For a change, it had been an exhausting day. The heavy, humid August heat made tempers flare, sane people crazy and the crime rate rise.

He walked into the station, as always surprised at the peace and quiet that night brought. In Chicago the station house had always been bright and frantic, no matter what the time. But here the lights were dimmed, the phone silent, and David, the man on duty, sat at his desk drinking a cup of coffee. He raised a hand in greeting to Russ, then returned his attention to his newspaper.

Russ stifled a yawn and dropped his daily reports on his desk, then headed for the storage room to grab some extra forms for the next day. He stopped in the doorway, shocked to see Bonnie seated at the desk, her head cradled on her folded arms, resting on the typewriter. He could hear her breaths coming slow and regular and knew she was deeply asleep.

Why hadn't she gone home? What was she doing here so late? The answer was obvious as he looked down. Crumpled forms littered the floor and overflowed the trash can. He smiled. Apparently the princess typist didn't type as well as she talked.

He leaned against the doorjamb, taking a moment to study her while she was quiet, vulnerable, unguarded. Her lashes were long and dark, casting shadows on her smooth, tanned cheeks. Without the energy and spunkiness she normally radiated, she seemed softer, more approachable.

His eyes narrowed as he scanned the length of her. What was it about her that caused his blood to thicken? Made him think erotic thoughts completely out of character for him? She didn't have the build of a sex siren—her breasts were too small, her hips too slender. She had a smart mouth, a wicked grin and an irreverence for all he held dear. So why did he want her?

"Bonnie?" He touched her shoulder gently. She didn't move, didn't stir at all. He shook her shoulder more forcefully. "Bonnie, wake up. You need to go home."

Her eyelids fluttered, then opened. Her gaze was dazed, disoriented. "Sam?" She sat up, the bewildered expression fading as consciousness claimed her. "Oh, wow." She rubbed her eyes, then looked at Russ. "What time is it?"

"After eleven." He leaned back against the doorjamb, watching as she reached to massage the back of her neck.

"Shoot, I was hoping to surprise Brenda Jo in the morning and have all these forms typed up." She stared at the stack still remaining.

"Come on, you can finish up tomorrow. It's late."

"You're right. I'm too tired to think anymore." She grabbed her purse and stood up, and together they said good-night to Dave and walked out into the sweet-smelling night air.

"I'll go with you," Russ said, not wanting her on the streets alone at night.

She pursed her lips, about to protest. Instead she swallowed. "I'd appreciate it."

He raised an eyebrow. "No argument? You must be tired."

"Just fighting the aftermath of a dream," she replied as they started down the sidewalk.

"About your brother?" he ventured, and she looked at him sharply. "You said his name when I first woke you up," he explained.

"What do you know about Sam?" she asked, her tone guarded.

"I know he's a suspect in your father's murder case. I know Carolyn believes he's innocent and in danger. Beau is conducting an unofficial investigation and trying to find him."

"Then you know pretty much what I know."

"So, what did you dream about?" As they passed beneath the glow of a street lamp, he saw the frown that creased her brow, and no trace of her usual bravado.

Despite the heat of the night, she wrapped her arms around herself, as if escaping the waltzing fingers of a shiver up her spine. "I've had the same dream almost every night since arriving here. Sam is running down a highway, and he keeps shouting back at me, trying to warn me about something, but I can't hear him. I can't understand him and I wake up scared for me . . . scared for him."

She squeezed her shoulders a final time, then allowed her arms to drop back at her sides. "It's no big deal. Caro told me Sam was seen walking down the highway outside of Casey's Corners. I'm sure that information is what makes me dream about it." She gazed up at Russ, a devilish spark in her eyes. "So, Caped Crusader, did you catch all the bad guys today?"

Any other time her mocking tone would have irritated him, but he recognized it for what it was—a place to hide the fear her dream had left behind. His sudden insight made her seem softer, more vulnerable. "I managed to keep the streets safe for the time being." He was sorry to realize they were in front of Carolyn and Beau's house.

"I think I can make it the rest of the way on my own," she said. "Thanks for escorting me." She turned to walk up the sidewalk to the front door.

Before she had gone two steps, Russ stopped her by quietly calling her name. She turned back to him, her eyes luminous in the moonlight, her mouth soft and warm looking. He hadn't known why he'd called her back until that moment. Then he understood. He wanted to kiss her, taste those sweet, sexy lips just once. And he could tell by the look in her eyes she realized exactly why he'd stopped her, exactly what he wanted.

She didn't resist when he pulled her into his arms. He knew it was madness, knew it was probably the dumbest thing he would ever do. But her scent whirled around him, banishing good sense, and her lips parted, inviting him into insanity. He lowered his mouth, wanting to claim hers, but just before their lips could touch, she raised a hand to block the kiss.

"No," she said softly, her eyes gleaming wickedly. "You want to be kissed way too badly for me to comply."

Before he could respond, she danced out of his arms and up the sidewalk. When she reached the front door she waved and blew him a kiss.

Despite his frustration, despite the utter aggravation, Russ laughed. He couldn't help it. She'd used his own words against him. She'd bested him, and he knew it, accepted it.

As he turned to walk home, he stopped laughing abruptly. He liked her, and at the moment the feelings rushing through him had little to do with physical desire. She made him laugh and he liked her. That scared the hell out of him.

Chapter Five

"What are your plans for today?" Carolyn asked Bonnie as she fed the twins their breakfast.

"I don't know. I'm almost sorry it's Saturday and I don't have to go to work." Bonnie grinned as Brent smeared pancake syrup through his hair. "Do you always have to give them baths after they eat?"

"Always." Carolyn laughed, then sobered and looked at Bonnie affectionately. "Have I told you lately how proud I am of you?"

Warmth blossomed in Bonnie's heart at her sister's words. How many years had she longed to hear somebody say that to her? It made her feel better than any shopping spree, warmer than drinking a dozen bottles of champagne. "I like working," she answered simply. "And my typing is getting better and better."

"I think it's wonderful that you're finally taking control of your life." Carolyn set the boys' plates in the sink. "Okay, guys, bath time." She got each of the kids out of their high chairs. "I'll be back in a few minutes."

"No hurry. I'm going to have another cup of coffee." When Carolyn and the kids left the kitchen, Bonnie got up and poured herself more coffee, then returned to the table.

Sounds of little boys giggling and Carolyn's loving murmurs came from the direction of the bathroom. Family sounds. Happy sounds. Helmut hadn't wanted children—in fact had abhorred children—and that was part of what had made Bonnie run from marrying him.

She wanted a family, a big family. She wanted to be the kind of mother she'd never had; wanted a house full of laughter and love. *It's wonderful that you're finally taking control of your life.* Bonnie sipped her coffee, thinking of her sister's words. Was that what she was doing?

After a week of working at the station, she had to admit she liked it. Brenda Jo had become a good friend and Beau was a wonderful boss. But how long would it be before that old restlessness struck her, before the core of loneliness that was always with her forced her to move on, seeking whatever it was that drove her, whatever it was she needed?

She sipped from her mug, her thoughts turning to Russ. Since the night he had walked her home, she'd hardly seen him. It was as if he'd spent the remainder of the week consciously avoiding her. At first she'd wondered if she'd made him mad by not kissing him. But he hadn't acted mad... just distant.

Maybe he's met some sweet little small-town woman and no longer has any interest in kissing me or having anything else to do with me, she thought, fighting a wave of sudden depression.

Perhaps she should go shopping. She'd gotten paid the day before, and although it wasn't a lot of money, it was enough to buy something nice for Beau and Carolyn to thank them for their support.

Draining her mug, she stood up, decision made. Yes, a day of shopping was a perfect way to spend a hot Saturday. At least most of the stores in Casey's Corners were air-conditioned.

Minutes later, after telling Carolyn her plans, Bonnie took off for Main Street. The sun was bright and hot overhead and she was grateful for the light-weight sundress she wore. As she walked, she tried to think of something special she could buy her sister and Beau.

They seemed to have everything they needed for happiness just in the mere fact that they had each other. Bonnie had never seen two people who appeared so right for each other. She could only hope that someday she'd find the right man for herself, a man who could fill the holes in her heart, soothe the scars on her soul, make the lonely ache finally go away forever.

She shoved aside these thoughts, knowing they were only more silly dreams. She wasn't the type to settle down and have a family. How often had she been told that? She'd probably spend her life flitting from place to place until her entire inheritance was gone and she was too old for anything but a nursing home. It doesn't have to be that way, a small voice inside her head whispered. You could stay here, build a life, be a real aunt to those little twin boys.

"Shut up," she muttered, realizing she was only managing to give herself a headache.

It took her most of the morning to find a gift for Beau and Carolyn. She finally located the perfect gift in the drugstore. It was a delicate figurine of a man and a woman holding hands, a symbol of love and commitment. Although it ate up more than half her paycheck, Bonnie bought it, sure this was the perfect way to thank Beau and Caro for their support.

With shopping behind her, she decided to treat herself to a piece of pie. Entering Wanda's Diner, she slid onto one of the stools at the counter, glad the lunch crowd had already departed and the place was nearly empty.

"What can I get for you?" the chubby, older woman behind the counter asked.

"A piece of apple pie and a cup of coffee."

"Coming right up."

Bonnie watched as the waitress cut a generous slice and placed it in front of her. "Hmm, that looks wonderful!" she exclaimed.

"Just came out of the oven about fifteen minutes ago. Happens to be one of my specialties." The waitress poured Bonnie a cup of coffee, then propped her elbows on the counter and gazed at her curiously. "You're Carolyn's sister, right?"

"Right. I'm Bonnie."

"Nice to meet you. I'm Wanda, proud proprietress of this eating establishment." Wanda's eyes twinkled merrily. "The grapevine is running wild with rumors about you."

Bonnie swallowed a bite of the pie and grinned. "What kind of rumors?"

Wanda leaned closer. "I'll tell you what I've heard if you tell me if it's true."

Bonnie grinned again. "It's a deal."

"I heard you were a princess traveling incognito."

"Oh, my," Bonnie said with a laugh. "The gossips have been busy."

Wanda smiled and winked. "The electricity might go off, the water might quit working, but the gossips never rest in this town." She tilted her head, her gaze still openly curious. "I also heard you and the new deputy are an item of sorts."

"That's ridiculous," Bonnie scoffed, feeling a tinge of heat rising to her cheeks. "Barney Fife and I have nothing going on between us." She grinned at Wanda's raucous laughter. "Believe me, that man is far too conservative for me."

"He needs a mama for that son of his," Wanda observed. "He and the boy came in here to eat supper last night and that's one sad-looking little boy."

"I'm sure Russ will have no trouble finding someone in this town more suitable than me for that job," Bonnie said, ignoring a pang in her heart as she thought of Russ and his son.

"I 'spect you're right. He's a fine-looking fellow, and I've never met a woman yet who didn't have a secret love for a man in a police uniform."

"You've just met one," Bonnie said dryly. She grinned again. "And if you hear any more gossip about me being a princess traveling incognito, you just tell them it's true."

Wanda slapped the counter and laughed loudly. "I'll do it," she agreed.

Bonnie breathed a sigh of relief as the door opened and an old man sat down at the end of the counter and signaled for Wanda. The last thing she wanted was to eat her pie listening to Wanda extol Russ's dubious charms. Talk about a case of indigestion.

She finished her pie and coffee and left her money, including a generous tip, on the counter, then went back outside into the afternoon heat.

She'd gone only a few steps down the sidewalk, when something hit her in the back of the head. "Ouch!" She whirled around in time to see a young boy, a dirt clod in one hand and a look of surprise on his filthy face. Another large clod of dirt lay at her feet. "Hey, did you throw this at me?" She glared at the kid, who glared back, his chin raised belligerently. "Hello. I'm talking to you." She started toward him, a dull ache in the back of her head where his dirt bomb had connected.

"I don't have to answer you," he said, raising his chin higher. "I don't have to talk to you at all."

"Why would you want to hit me?" she asked, standing directly in front of him.

"I wasn't aiming at you. I wasn't aiming at anything."

Bonnie eyed the kid with irritation. He didn't seem a bit sorry. In fact, he looked like a future criminal. A young Al Capone. Or perhaps in this case Baby-face Nelson was more appropriate. Maybe it would be good for her to put a little scare into him. The police station was right across the street. Before he could guess her intention, she grabbed his wrist.

"Let me go!"

He kicked her, connecting with her ankle. She yelped in pain, but didn't release her hold.

"Let's go have a little talk with the sheriff. Maybe he can convince you how dangerous it is to throw things at people."

"Let me go, you ugly witch."

"Stop kicking me or I'll turn you into a toad," Bonnie threatened.

"If you do I'll give you warts," the kid returned.

"Then I'll bite off the warts and make a potion to turn you into...into..."Bonnie struggled for something a little boy would find abhorrent. She grinned triumphantly. "I'll turn you into a girl."

"You're crazy," he gasped as she dragged him across the street and into the station.

"What's going on?" Brenda Jo stood up from her desk as they entered.

"I'm here to make a citizen's spanking," Bonnie said, grimacing as the minimonster child kicked once again, this time connecting with her bag from the drugstore. There was an ominous crunch and Bonnie moaned, knowing the figurine had been destroyed. She placed the sack on the counter, still not relinquishing her grasp on the boy. "Where's Beau? I think this juvenile delinquent needs a word with the sheriff."

"I'll go get him." Before Brenda Jo could leave the room, Russ walked in.

"Daniel!" he exclaimed.

"Dad!" the little boy cried.

"Daniel?" Bonnie released her hold on the child, staring in surprise first at Russ, then at the kid. Of course. She should have seen the resemblance. Daniel's face was a miniature of Russ's, with the same lean

angles and deep cleft in his chin. This was the sad little boy Wanda had talked about? There was nothing
sad about this miniature whirlwind of trouble.

"What is going on?" Russ asked.

Daniel ran to his father and buried his head in his
midsection. "I didn't mean to. I didn't mean to hit
her."

Russ stroked his son's hair, looking at Bonnie for an
explanation.

"He nailed me in the back of the head with a dirt
clod and called me an ugly witch," she explained,
rather embarrassed about the entire incident. "I
probably overreacted, but I thought perhaps a talk
from you would teach him the dangers of throwing
things at people."

"I wasn't throwing at her—she just got in the way."
As his shoulders shook with sobs, Daniel tightened his
arms around his father.

Russ pulled the boy from him and held him by the
shoulders. "Daniel, you never throw dirt clods.
Somebody could get hurt. Now, turn around and
apologize to Miss Baker."

Daniel faced her. Although tears streaked down his
face, Bonnie saw the anger still radiating from his dark
eyes.

"I'm sorry," he said petulantly.

"Apology accepted," she replied.

"Sit down right here and wait for me," Russ instructed his son, then turned to Bonnie. "Come on, I'll walk you out."

"Bonnie, don't forget your bag," Brenda Jo said.

"Just throw it away. It's trashed." Bonnie walked outside with Russ. "I'm sorry I made such a big deal out of this," she began.

He held up his hand to still her. "No, I'm sorry Daniel hit you. He shouldn't have been throwing things."

She shrugged. "No real harm done." She refused to think of the loss of the figurine. She'd get another one when she got paid again.

"Bonnie, come to dinner tomorrow night."

She looked at him in surprise. He'd spent the past week seemingly avoiding her and suddenly he was inviting her to dinner?

Apparently he sensed her confusion. "Just a friendly dinner, a chance for Daniel to redeem himself. I can't stand the thought of him making such a bad first impression on anyone."

"Okay," she agreed. Why not? It would give Caro and Beau an opportunity to spend an evening alone.

"Great. I'll pick you up about six." Arrangements made, Russ watched as she walked away, her hips swaying saucily beneath the bright-pink sundress.

Why in the hell had he invited her to dinner? He'd spent the past week trying to keep her out of his mind, but it was a difficult task. The whole station smelled of her perfume, and often late in the afternoon before she got off work, he'd hear her laughter mingling with Brenda Jo's.

Before he'd married Anne, everyone had warned him that she was spoiled, selfish, not ready for the kind of commitment marriage entailed. But he hadn't listened. He'd been besotted with Anne's beauty, charmed by her lust for life. He hadn't realized the very qualities that had made him fall in love with her would eventually cause him to fall out of love.

He wasn't about to make the same mistake with Bonnie Baker. Although he was drawn to her, amused and charmed by her, he was wiser and smarter than he'd been years before.

The only reason he'd invited her to dinner was so she wouldn't think Daniel was a bad kid. He couldn't stand the thought of anyone thinking ill of his son. Daniel was his life.

He turned and went back into the station, satisfied with his simple motivation for asking her to dinner.

As he walked in, he saw Brenda Jo about to toss Bonnie's sack into the garbage. "Wait—why did she want that thrown away?"

Brenda Jo looked at him uneasily. "Whatever it is, it was broken in the fracas between Bonnie and Daniel."

"Daniel broke it?"

"He was trying to get away from Bonnie and sort of kicked it. He didn't break it intentionally."

"Still, the fact remains he broke it. I'll replace whatever it is and take it out of Daniel's allowance." He retrieved the sack from Brenda Jo, wondering what the princess had bought for herself with her first paycheck. Expensive perfume? A piece of jewelry?

He opened the sack and pulled out three pieces of a figurine. "It's definitely broken," he said, fitting the pieces together to see what the object had been. There was also a card. He pulled it out and realized the delicate piece had been meant as a gift for Carolyn and Beau.

Damn. It irritated him. He'd assumed the first item she'd buy would be some fancy something for herself. Why did she have to go and do something so totally out of character? Or was it possible he knew less about the princess's character than he thought he did?

"This is the first time I've seen you without your clothes," Bonnie said as she and Russ walked to his car the next evening. She laughed at his raised eyebrow. "I mean without your cop clothes," she amended.

"Sundays are always T-shirt-and-jeans days." He opened the passenger door for her. "I hope you like spaghetti."

"Love it," she answered, sliding into the seat and watching as he walked around the front of the car to the driver's side. She couldn't help but notice he looked good in the worn jeans and pale-blue T-shirt.

The jeans hugged his slender hips and the short-sleeved shirt exposed bulging biceps she hadn't noticed before. She wished she hadn't noticed them now.

He slid behind the wheel and started the engine. "I left Daniel and Mrs. Garfield, the neighbor, in charge of the garlic bread. Let's hope he remembered to take it out of the oven or we'll be eating garlic-flavored ashes."

"I'm sure it will be fine. I'm just impressed that you can cook."

"I couldn't before my divorce, but I learned quick enough that Daniel and I shouldn't live on fast food alone. Besides, I like to cook. It gives me a sense of accomplishment."

Bonnie nodded with a grin. "Probably the same feeling I get whenever I order room service." It was the kind of answer she knew he expected of her, one she knew would make him laugh. Sure enough, she was rewarded with his rich laughter filling the car.

"At times I find it impossible to believe that you and Carolyn had the same parents. The two of you seem so different," he finally said.

"Oh, we aren't so different," Bonnie replied thoughtfully. "We just learned to cope with things differently."

"Cope with what?"

Bonnie shrugged, refusing to be drawn into painful memories of growing up feeling unloved, unwanted, the heartache of knowing she would never live up to her father's expectations. It had been so much easier to live up to his disappointments. "Oh, you know, the usual childhood-trauma stuff." She shot him a cheeky grin. "It was horrible having to wait until I was sixteen to get my first gold charge card."

"Hmm, I'm surprised it didn't scar you for life." He pulled into the driveway of an attractive, two-story house. "This is it."

"Russ, this is really nice," Bonnie said as she got out of the car and perused the structure. The evening sun cast golden light on the pale blue house with navy shutters. Flowers bloomed in riotous colors near the wide porch, scenting the air with sweet fragrance. A porch swing swayed gently in the warm breeze, inviting a body to sit and rest awhile.

"It needs repainting, and a couple of the shutters are about to fall off, but by the end of the summer I should have everything taken care of," he explained as they walked to the front door.

"Hmm, something smells wonderful." The air was pungent with the scent of spicy tomato sauce.

"Let's hope it tastes as good as it smells. Daniel, Mrs. Garfield, we're back," he called, then motioned to the sofa. "Why don't you have a seat and I'll chase down Daniel and Mrs. Garfield?" He disappeared up the staircase.

Bonnie looked around with interest. She hadn't really known what to expect, but she hadn't anticipated the warmth and homey atmosphere. The furniture was

Southwestern, in colors of rose, cactus and peach. The end tables gleamed with a high polish, and Indian artwork hung framed on the walls.

The room was clean, with just enough clutter to look lived in. Video games were scattered directly in front of the television, two baseball mitts rested near a lamp.

Bonnie walked over to a built-in, wooden bookcase, noting that most of the books on the shelves were mysteries and police procedurals. A row of photos drew her attention, photos of Russ and Daniel in various poses together. She picked up one of father and son holding fishing poles, a sparkling lake visible behind them. Daniel looked to be about five, his face open and smiling, without a hint of the anger she'd seen in him the day before.

She touched a fingertip to Russ's face. Funny, she'd thought of him only in terms of his job. Russ, the by-the-book cop who'd ticketed her for speeding. Russ, the officer whose gaze held a touch of disapproval when he looked at her. She hadn't given much thought to Russ the father... Russ the man. She put the picture away, uncomfortable with these new thoughts. She didn't want to imagine him having wants and needs, entertaining dreams and hopes. It made him too human, too real. She whirled around as Russ came back down the stairs.

"Hmm, they must be out back. Come on, you've got to see the perfect climbing tree that came with the place."

Following him through the kitchen, she was again struck with the coziness of the place. The kitchen was bright and cheerful, decorated boldly in red and black. She knew immediately that this room was the real heart of the house. A portable television sat on the counter and childish drawings of jungle animals hung by magnets on the refrigerator door. It was easy to imagine father and son seated at the table, indulging in small talk that meant nothing to anyone but themselves. The room implied an intimacy only a family could share, and for a moment Bonnie envied Daniel. He was lucky to have one parent who obviously loved him.

Russ motioned to the loaf of bread on the top of the stove. "At least they remembered to take it out." He opened the back door. "And if I know my kid, he's in the tree. He's been spending all his spare time up there."

As they walked outside and Bonnie saw the tree, she understood why Daniel spent time up in the leafy branches. It was a beautiful tree, a huge oak with limbs perfect for climbing. An older woman with short, curly gray hair sat in a lawn chair at the base of the tree, a worried frown deepening the wrinkles on her forehead.

Russ quickly introduced Bonnie to his neighbor, who, he explained, watched Daniel for him whenever Russ needed her to. "I told him not to climb the tree without you being here," Mrs. Garfield declared. "But Daniel wouldn't listen to me."

"It's fine, Mrs. Garfield. Thanks for coming over." Russ smiled warmly at her. With a nod to both of them, Mrs. Garfield left.

"Daniel, Miss Baker is here. It's time to come down and wash up for dinner."

"I'm not hungry," Daniel's voice drifted down from the top of the tree. "I don't wanna come down."

Russ shot Bonnie an apologetic look. "First the divorce and his mother leaving, then the move... it's been hard on him." He walked to the bottom of the tree. "Daniel, Bonnie is our guest."

There was a moment of silence, then the rustle of leaves as Daniel descended the tree. He landed on his feet in front of them, his face smudged with dirt and his dark, curly hair in disarray.

"I'd say a bath is in order before dinner," Russ observed.

Daniel opened his mouth, obviously to protest.

"A bath," Russ repeated firmly.

"How about something to drink?" Russ asked when they were back in the kitchen, Bonnie seated at the table, with Daniel upstairs taking a bath. "I've got some red wine."

"Sounds good," Bonnie replied. "Can I help do anything?"

"No. It will just take a minute for me to boil the spaghetti." He poured her a glass of the wine, placed a large pot of water on the stove, then joined her at the table. "Brenda Jo tells me you're doing a good job helping her at the station."

Something about the setting, the coziness of the kitchen, the intimacy of sitting next to Russ scared her. "It's something to do until the next inheritance check comes," she replied flippantly, then instantly wished she could recall the words.

"Yeah, I'll bet you can't wait to jump on a jet and get out of this provincial town," he said dryly, his eyes darkening.

"At the moment I'm in no hurry to leave Casey's Corners." She sipped her wine, looking at him thoughtfully. "Why did you invite me to dinner tonight? It can't be because you wanted to spend time with me—it's obvious you don't like me very much."

He flushed slightly, disconcerted by her question. "I didn't like the fact that you'd gotten a negative impression of Daniel, and, I have to admit, you fascinate me, Princess."

"You must fascinate easily," she returned with a wry grin.

"And I know why you agreed to have dinner with me." He stood and returned to the pot of now-boiling water, and efficiently added the noodles. "You're fascinated with me, too."

Bonnie nearly spit out her mouthful of wine at his confident words. Before she could recover, he continued.

"I figure it's the old thing of opposites attracting." He turned back and looked at her, his gaze assessing. "Of course, if we ever decided to do anything crazy like date, we'd probably kill each other inside of a week."

Bonnie laughed. "As if I'd ever agree to date you in the first place."

"As if I'd ask you in the first place," he countered.

"Is it time to eat?" Daniel walked into the kitchen, his presence effectively stopping their contentious conversation.

Dinner was an odd experience. Daniel alternated between sullenness and belligerence. She was surprised Russ never lost his temper, never raised his voice with the boy. The spaghetti was superb, and Russ kept her entertained with stories about the lighter side of his police work in Chicago.

She envied him the pride he took in his work, the sense of purpose that obviously filled his life. They talked about politics, and as a staunch liberal she wasn't surprised to discover him a loyal conservative.

"Why don't you two go in and play a video game while I clean up the dishes?" Russ suggested when they had finished eating.

"Oh, no, I should help with cleanup," she protested.

He grinned. "I've seen you dry dishes, and it wasn't a pretty sight. Besides, you're my guest. Go on, get out of here."

Reluctantly Bonnie followed Daniel into the living room, where he inserted a game into the video machine and handed her a paddle. "You like to play video games?" she asked brightly.

He shrugged, not dignifying her with an answer. Instead he focused his attention on the TV screen.

"So what do you like to do besides play video games?" she asked, once again trying to make conversation. Again he ignored her. "Is there anything else you like to do when you aren't being a social butterfly?"

"You're dumb."

Bonnie grinned. "I'm not too dumb—I made you talk."

He scowled. "You're stupid."

"And you're rude," she countered. "But that's okay. There are moments when I'm rude, too."

They took turns playing the game for a few minutes in silence, and she felt him glower at her several times. He was definitely an unpleasant kid, Bonnie thought. He didn't even attempt to be civil to her. She wondered if he was unpleasant to everyone or if it was something personal with her. When she was about to beat his score, he abruptly shut off the machine. He leaned back against the sofa and glared at her.

"I don't like you," he stated.

"You aren't exactly impressing me, either."

He nodded slightly, almost as if he was satisfied with her answer. "I'm going up to my room." Without another word, he stood and raced up the stairs.

Bonnie sat for a long moment, wondering if eight was too young to induct a boy into the army. The kid could definitely use some discipline or something. Thank goodness it wasn't her problem.

She looked up as Russ came in. "What happened to Daniel?" he asked.

"He had some things he wanted to do in his room. I told him to go ahead." Bonnie wasn't about to tattle on the kid for his poor manners.

"How about a cup of coffee out on the swing?" Russ suggested.

"That sounds great."

"Let me just check on Daniel, then I'll bring the coffee outside."

Bonnie walked out the front door as Russ went up the stairs. The sun had set, pulling a blanket of darkness onto the sky. There were no stars, and the air was thick and heavy, scented with flowers and the underlying promise of a late-night storm.

Sitting down on the swing, Bonnie wondered what she was doing there. Why was she having coffee with a man she wasn't sure she liked, a man who didn't seem to realize he had the child from hell?

She'd done some crazy things in her life. Two years before she'd run with the bulls in Spain. She'd scuba-dived in shark-infested waters and parachuted out of a tiny plane that had been going down. But none of those seemed as crazy as her being here in Russ's house. Those other things had placed her body at risk, but being here with Russ somehow threatened her heart, and that was something she'd never before allowed. Always before, if she'd felt her heart getting involved, she'd run as fast and as far away as possible.

You're being ridiculous, she chided inwardly. Her heart wasn't about to become involved with Russ and his wayward kid. Russ had said it earlier: what she felt was a certain attraction to an opposite. She was fascinated by him, but certainly not about to become involved emotionally with him.

He stepped outside, a mug of coffee in each hand. "Hmm, smells like rain," he murmured as he held out one of the mugs to her.

When she'd taken it, he eased down beside her on the swing, his thigh pressed warmly against her own. "Maybe the rain will cool things off," she replied, trying to ignore the heat that swept over her, that had nothing to do with the night air and everything to do with Russ's closeness.

"August rains seldom cool things off." Russ leaned back in the swing, causing it to sway gently.

"Tell me about your family, Russ. Are your parents still alive?" She wanted conversation, anything to distract her from his closeness.

"There isn't much to tell. My father is dead, but my mom lives in Chicago, in the same house where I was born."

"Are you close to her?"

He grinned. "She threatens to ground me if I don't call her at least once a week." He looked at her for a long moment. "I gather you weren't close to your parents."

Bonnie laughed, recognizing a touch of bitterness in her laughter. "I was closer to the cook, and she hated me." She took a sip of her coffee and stared reflectively at the night-blackened sky. "I didn't seem to fit anywhere. Sam was the only son and followed my father into his business. Carolyn worked her tail off to gain Father's respect by also going into the business. Colleen was the baby, and probably the smartest of us all. She turned her back on the entire Baker empire. She's now a social worker on Long Island."

She shrugged and laughed again. "It's no big deal. We all managed to survive without our parents' love and nurturing." Raising her chin slightly, she eyed Russ defiantly. "I learned not to need anyone except Garrison."

"Garrison?"

Bonnie grinned. "Garrison Fielder, my father's partner and the one who cuts my inheritance checks."

Russ shook his head. "What on earth would you have done if you hadn't been born rich?"

"I would have learned to travel coach instead of first-class."

He laughed, then drained his cup of coffee and set it on the porch next to the swing. "Oh, Princess."

The laughter faded and instead of mirth, desire darkened his eyes. Before she had time to prepare, or even guess his intentions, his lips descended toward hers as his arms enfolded her and drew her nearer.

His mouth moved hungrily against hers. There was nothing tentative, nothing hesitant, in the way his lips claimed hers. She tasted his hunger, and it evoked a like emotion in her. Allowing her coffee cup to drop to the porch with a thud, she wound her arms around him. He moaned, his tongue deepening the kiss as his hands tangled in her hair.

Heat suffused her, centering in a ball of flames in the pit of her stomach as his tongue danced with hers in a battle of raw desire. It was a kiss like no other Bonnie had ever experienced. It jangled every nerve ending, banished every other thought out of her mind, stirred her very soul.

Finally he drew away from her, and Bonnie stared at him. "Oh, my," she managed to gasp. She stood up and stumbled to the edge of the porch. "I . . . I think I'd better get home."

"Bonnie, don't go." He leaned forward and raked a hand through his hair, then looked at her again. "I don't think either of us can deny there's something strong between us." He held up a hand to still her protest, then stood up and approached her. "Bonnie, I felt your heartbeat racing when I kissed you."

"You caught me off guard, that's all."

"Is this your usual habit, Bonnie? To stir up a man, then run?"

"I'm not running," she protested. "I'm just going home. It's late, and I'm tired." She flushed as he eyed her knowingly.

He sighed in defeat. "Let me get my keys. I'll drive you back."

"That's not necessary. It's not that far, and I really feel like walking." She moved down the porch steps to the sidewalk. "Thanks for dinner, Russ."

"Sure." He leaned against the banister, his eyes glittering darkly in the night. "Bonnie, it was just a kiss."

"I know that," she snapped.

"It wasn't a proposal of marriage or anything like that."

"Like I'd accept a proposal of marriage from you," she retorted.

"Like I'd offer one." He snorted disdainfully.

She refused to dignify his answer with a response. Instead she whirled around and headed down the street. She slowed her footsteps, refusing to let him see her hurry away, not wanting him to notice that she was in any way affected by his kiss. Drat the man anyway. He was the most arrogant, obnoxious man she'd ever met.

When his house was out of sight, she picked up her pace, anger giving way to wonder. Who would have thought it? She touched her lips, remembering the heat, the hunger, of his kiss. Who would have thought that a briefs kind of guy would kiss like a wild and crazy boxers fellow?

Chapter Six

"How was dinner last night?" Carolyn asked.

"Fine." Bonnie eyed the toaster irritably, wondering why there were mornings when it seemed to take forever for the bread to pop up.

"Just *fine?*" Carolyn eyed her curiously.

"He fixed spaghetti. It was good. We ate, then I came home." The bread popped up and Bonnie grabbed it. She busied herself buttering it, ignoring Caro's speculative gaze. She carried the toast to the table and plopped down across from her sister. "It wasn't a date—it wasn't a big deal."

Carolyn sipped her coffee, her gaze remaining on Bonnie. "Is somebody a little cranky this morning?"

"I suppose I am a little," Bonnie agreed with an apologetic smile. "I'm really tired. I didn't sleep well last night." She took a bite of toast. "It must have been the storm."

"It was quite a storm," Carolyn agreed. "I didn't know the wind could blow so hard. I heard on the radio a little while ago that electrical lines are down all over town. I'm glad we have power."

"I know the wind was fierce. I was afraid I'd wake up in the munchkinland."

At that moment the twins yelled from their room. Carolyn laughed and stood up. "Ah, speaking of munchkins, there they are now. I'll be back in a few minutes." She left the kitchen and disappeared down the hallway.

Bonnie ate quickly, glancing at the clock and realizing it was time for her to leave for work. She went into the twins' bedroom, where Carolyn was changing Trent's diaper, while Brent jabbered and jumped impatiently in his crib. "I've got to get to work. I'll see you tonight."

"Would you do a favor for me?" Carolyn finished the diapering.

"If the favor has anything to do with me touching that dirty diaper, the answer is no."

Carolyn laughed and tossed the soiled diaper in the trash can. "I'm planning a barbecue next weekend for Beau's birthday. Sunday afternoon, around two o'clock. Would you invite Russ and Daniel for me?"

Bonnie controlled the frown that tried to take over her features. "Why me? Can't you just call him or something?"

Carolyn looked at her in surprise. "I just thought you could mention it when you see Russ at work today, but if you don't want to, I'll call him."

"No, it's okay," Bonnie replied, realizing she'd overreacted to a simple request. "Don't worry, I'll take care of it. See you tonight." Waving a quick goodbye, she left the house.

As she walked down the sidewalk, evidence of the late-night storm was everywhere. Leaves littered the ground, pounded by rain or blown out of the trees. Despite the fact that the rain hadn't cooled things off, a fresh, clean scent hung in the air. She took a deep breath, filling her lungs with the sweetness.

Bonnie had lied when she'd told her sister the storm had kept her awake. In reality, it had been the kiss. That damnable kiss had kept her tossing and turning all night long. It had sparked with electricity, snapped with energy and touched her like no other she'd ever experienced. The fierce storm that had raged for over an hour in the middle of the night couldn't compare with the intensity of that damned kiss. There had been nothing artful in Russ's kiss, only raw emotion that had demanded a response. And God, how she had responded.

Even now the memory had the power to curl her toes, weaken her knees, warm her throughout. She kicked at a rain-sodden leaf in her path.

Russ had said last night that something was obviously at work between them, something powerful. Lust? Certainly she felt a physical attraction to the man. Was it more than mere physical attraction?

As much as she hated to, she had to admit she liked his wit. Few men in her life had been able to spar verbally with her and win.

As the station came into view, she slowed her footsteps. Thank God she wouldn't have to face Russ until two, when he came on duty. By then she would have a tight rein on her emotions. She'd run last night, confused by the feelings his kiss had evoked. Her head was clearer this morning, despite her lack of sleep. She could accept the fact that she was physically attracted to Russ, but she knew she could allow the attraction to go no further, no deeper, than sheer lust.

She and Russ were all wrong for each other. Hell, if put in a room alone together for an hour, they'd probably kill each other...or make delicious love. Her mind filled with a vision of the two of them naked and in each other's arms. "Stop it," she hissed to her traitorous mind as she walked into the station.

"Okay, I'll stop," Brenda Jo said. "But what am I supposed to stop?"

Bonnie laughed. "Nothing. I was talking to myself." She looked at Brenda Jo curiously. In the past week of working together, she and Brenda Jo had discussed many things, but Brenda had never mentioned a husband or boyfriend. "Brenda Jo, do you have a significant other?"

Brenda Jo frowned. "A significant other what?"

"You know... husband, boyfriend, important person in your life, lover."

"Sure, I've got a boyfriend." Her cheeks flushed an uncharacteristic pink. "You know Lloyd Kingburg?"

"The produce guy at the grocery store?" Bonnie asked incredulously.

Brenda Jo nodded, her blush deepening. "We've been seeing each other for almost five years. We're planning on getting married as soon as we can afford it. Right now Lloyd is putting three of his children through college and he refuses to marry me until he can give me a honeymoon in Paris." She tilted her head and eyed Bonnie curiously. "Why all the questions? You having man trouble?"

"Hardly. I don't have a man to give me trouble."

"That's not what I hear." Brenda Jo grinned knowingly.

"Whatever you've heard, it's not true. That kiss between Russ and me meant absolutely nothing."

Brenda Jo's eyebrows bounced up in surprise. "Honey, the gossip I heard isn't half as juicy as your confession."

Bonnie's face warmed. She should have just kept her mouth shut. "Just pretend I didn't say anything, okay?"

Brenda Jo leaned back in her chair and grinned. "I'm not sure I can do that. I'd like to hear more about this kiss that didn't mean anything. Sounds to me like a case of the lady protesting too much."

"Don't be ridiculous. I've got typing to do," Bonnie replied, escaping into the storage room, with Brenda Jo's laughter following her.

Rolling a clean form into the typewriter, Bonnie shoved all memories of Russ and the kiss out of her head. She didn't have time to entertain thoughts of a man who was totally inappropriate for her. There was absolutely no future in falling into any kind of a relationship with Russ.

She worked without stop for the next hour, pleased with the progress she'd made with the stack of forms. Deciding to take a break and get a cup of coffee from the community pot in the back room, she left her desk. She yelped in surprise as she bumped into Russ's broad chest.

"Whoa."

He caught her by her upper arms, his fingers lingering with warmth against her bare skin. "What are you doing here so early?" she asked, flustered by his unexpected appearance.

"Beau called me and asked me to cover for him. He's going out to help with some of the downed trees from the storm last night."

His gaze roved her face, lingering on her mouth, and she knew he was remembering their kiss. As his thumbs moved in tiny circles against her skin, she stepped away from him.

"Running away again, Bonnie?" he asked, amusement quirking his lips.

"Don't be ridiculous," she scoffed. "I was just on my way to get some coffee." She scooted past him, irritated when he followed her.

In the tiny back room that served as a combination break room and kitchenette, she went directly to the coffee maker and filled her cup. When she turned around he stood right in front of her.

"You look tired," he observed. "Didn't you sleep well?" He grinned. "Maybe you need to check beneath your mattress for a pea, Princess."

"I slept fine." She lifted her chin and smiled. "The deep, dreamless sleep of the innocent."

He chuckled. "Now, why do I find that hard to believe?"

Bonnie shrugged, too tired, too confused, to spar with him. "I've got to get back to work." She scooted around him, then turned back to him once again. "By the way, Carolyn is having a barbecue next Sunday for Beau's birthday. She'd like you and Daniel to come."

"Sounds good. What time?"

"Around two."

He grinned again, the teasing gesture that set Bonnie's teeth on edge.

"Is this a date?"

"Hmm, like I'd ask you for a date," she scoffed.

"Like I'd accept," he countered, then grinned again, obviously enjoying their little verbal game.

With an exasperated sigh she turned and left. He watched as she went down the corridor and disappeared into the storage room. He was sorry she'd slept well. He'd hoped she'd tossed and turned as he had, playing and replaying their kiss in her mind.

He walked over to the coffeepot and poured himself a cup, wondering what he was going to do about his lustful feelings for Bonnie Baker.

He'd known kissing her would be a major mistake, but damned if he could control the urge. And sure enough, it had been. Because he wanted to repeat the mistake... again and again and again.

Maybe an affair with her was just what he needed. A hot, brief affair that would get his desire for her out of his system once and for all. It made sense—rather than fighting his passion, to go with it, allow it to take over. It sounded wonderful, thrilling, but he knew he wouldn't do it.

Sipping his coffee, he walked back to his desk and sat down, his mind still unclear about what he wanted from Bonnie. He'd never been the type of man to contemplate a relationship without emotional commitment. And he knew the price he'd pay for an emotional commitment to somebody as weak, as fickle, as Bonnie. That price was too high.

If he was smart, he'd stay away from her. Refuse to get involved on any level. Within a couple of months Bonnie would get her next inheritance check and she'd be gone. Yes, if he was smart he'd keep his distance. He'd made one big mistake with Anne. He wasn't about to make another.

He leaned back in his chair and closed his eyes. For once in his life it would be nice if he could be a wild and crazy boxers man and follow his hormones without the involvement of his heart.

"I can't believe Beau is so late getting home," Carolyn said, for the third time in an hour walking over to the front window and peering out into the twilight.

"There must have been a lot of damage from the storm," Bonnie replied. She sat in the center of the living room, the twins next to her and a pile of building blocks before them. "Come sit down and stop being a worrywart. I'm sure he'll be home soon."

Carolyn sank back down on the sofa, a frown still creasing the center of her forehead. "The roast is going to be all dried out," she said, more to herself than to anyone.

Bonnie grinned. "Most of your roasts usually are." She ducked as Carolyn threw a decorative pillow at her. As Bonnie built a block tower with the boys, her thoughts turned to Russ. Thankfully she had managed to avoid him for most of the day, but she was still so confused where he was concerned.

She couldn't deny she felt something for him, something she'd never felt before. A part of her wanted to allow things to play out, see where it carried them. Another part of her wanted to run . . . fast and far away.

She looked up, drawn from her thoughts as Carolyn jumped off the sofa.

"I've got to do something. Want a glass of iced tea?"

"Sure," Bonnie agreed. As Carolyn disappeared into the kitchen, Bonnie turned her attention back to the kids. She pulled Brent into her lap, smelling his fresh, clean scent. He leaned against her, so trusting, so completely accepting. She thought of Daniel, his features hardened with belligerence, his eyes angry and mistrustful.

Whoever eventually married Russ would have her hands full with that child. Did Russ even realize his son was a problem? Couldn't he see that Daniel needed some hard and fast discipline? Bonnie loved children, but she had a feeling even Mother Teresa would have problems loving a kid like Daniel.

"Here you go." Carolyn reentered with two glasses of tea.

Bonnie sat Brent back on the floor, then stood up and took the drink. "While Beau is gone, why don't

we make plans for his birthday barbecue?'' she suggested, hoping to take Carolyn's mind off Beau's
lateness.

"Did you ask Russ today about coming?"

Bonnie nodded. "He said he and Daniel would be
here."

She sat down on the sofa and motioned for Carolyn to sit beside her. "So who else are you inviting to
this barbecue?"

"Waylon and his family, and of course Brenda Jo."

"Did you know she dates Lloyd Kingburg?"

"Lloyd Kingburg? You mean the older man who
works in the grocery store? The one who blushes every
time anyone asks him a question?" Bonnie nodded
and they both giggled. Carolyn shook her head and
laughed again. "It's just hard to believe. Brenda Jo is
so colorful, so bold, and Lloyd seems so shy and
timid."

"You know what they say about opposites attracting," Bonnie remarked, then sobered as she realized
that's exactly what Russ had said to explain the attraction they felt for each other.

For the next half hour the two sisters discussed the
rest of the guest list and the menu for the birthday
barbecue. "Beau loves ribs, and Waylon has promised to be in charge of the cooking. I'm ordering the
potato salad and baked beans, and we'll have chips
and relishes," Carolyn explained.

"Stop. You're making me hungry," Bonnie replied. Both of them jumped as a knock sounded at the front door. "I'll get it," she said. She opened the door and stepped back in surprise. "Russ!"

Carolyn stood up from the sofa as Russ stepped inside. Her hand flew to her mouth as she looked at the unsmiling man. "Oh, God, it's Beau, isn't it? Something has happened to him."

"No! No, Beau is fine," Russ hurriedly reassured her. "He's over at the Briggs Funeral Home. He was out in a field helping with some downed lines, and... well... they found a body."

Russ looked distinctly uncomfortable, and Bonnie's heart thudded in apprehension.

"Russ, why are you here?" Bonnie finally asked.

He appeared pained, his gaze going from Bonnie to Carolyn, then back again. "The man we found...he's been dead for a while...stabbed. We found his identification in his wallet. We're afraid it's...Sam."

Carolyn cried out, and Bonnie reached for her, needing to hang on to her sister as Russ's words slowly sank in. Sam dead? The words whirled in Bonnie's head as Carolyn sobbed against her shoulder. Russ became a blur as Bonnie's eyes filled, although not before she saw compassion softening his features.

He cleared his throat and shifted from foot to foot. "I need one of you to come with me to make a positive identification."

Carolyn raised her head and stared at Bonnie in horror. "I don't think I can," she whispered.

"It's all right. You don't have to. I'll go." Bonnie drew a deep breath, fingers of dread walking up her spine. She didn't want to do this—dear God, she didn't want to. She wanted to hop on a plane, drive away in a car, anything that would keep her from dealing with this horror.

However, she wouldn't run. Carolyn needed her now, and for once in her life, Bonnie intended to do the right thing.

She led Carolyn back to the sofa. "You stay here with the kids. I'll take care of this." She leaned over and gave her sister a hug, then straightened and looked at Russ. "Let's get this over with."

Russ led her out to his car and she slid into the passenger seat, her mind still grappling with the idea that Sam was dead.

All the waiting and wondering about her brother's whereabouts, all the worry about his safety had been for naught. She closed her eyes, thinking of Sam's wife and their little girl. A wife without a husband. A daughter without her daddy. A tear spilled down her cheek. A sister without a brother.

The car pulled to a stop, the engine shut off, and still Bonnie kept her eyes closed, gathering strength for what lay ahead.

"You okay?"

Russ's voice was soft, his hand warm as he reached over and gently touched her shoulder.

She opened her eyes and nodded, staring at the funeral home in front of them. "Why did they bring him here?" she asked. "Don't they usually take . . . bodies to a morgue?"

Russ nodded. "Casey's Corners doesn't have a morgue. The city has an arrangement with the funeral home."

She drew in a deep, tremulous breath and opened her car door. "Let's go."

They were met at the door by Beau, who expressed surprise at seeing Bonnie instead of Carolyn. Russ understood his surprise. He, too, had just assumed Carolyn would be the one to make the identification.

"Bonnie . . . I'm sorry you have to do this," Beau said in greeting.

She nodded and gave him a quick hug. "Go home, Beau," she said as she released him. "Go home to Carolyn. Russ can take me in. Caro needs you with her."

Beau exchanged a questioning glance with Russ. "I'll handle things here," Russ replied. With a final hug to Bonnie, Beau took off for his car.

Russ placed his arm around Bonnie's shoulders, unable to fight his need to support her, comfort her. For a moment she leaned into him, as if drawing strength from his embrace. Russ tightened his arms around her, smelling the scent of her clean hair, as he felt a tremor shake through her.

She finally pulled away from him, her chin lifted in the now-familiar gesture of boldness. "Come on, let's get this over with." Not waiting for him, she strode through the front door, her posture rigid with determination.

Russ followed behind, admiring Bonnie's courage, her strength. She could have insisted Carolyn come— in truth, that's what he'd expected. It had surprised him to see Carolyn fall apart and Bonnie be the strong one. Once again he realized Bonnie had risen above his expectations, and it unsettled him.

When they entered the funeral home, Russ led Bonnie down a flight of stairs. Before taking her into the room where the body was kept, he picked up an item from a nearby table and held it out to Bonnie. "Can you tell me if this is your brother's?" he asked.

She opened the tanned, leather wallet and sagged against the wall. Russ already knew what was inside—a wad of money, several credit cards and a picture of a woman and a little, dark-haired girl. She caught her bottom lip between her teeth as she stared at the photograph. When she looked up at Russ, her eyes were huge, sparkling with tears she seemed to hold back by mere stubbornness alone.

"This is Sam's wife and his daughter."

Russ nodded and took the wallet from her. He handed her a gold wedding band. "What about this?"

She studied it, noting the initials engraved on the inside. "Yes...yes, it's Sam's."

The tears sparkled more brightly, clinging to her lashes and causing Russ's heart to ache for her.

"Bonnie, I don't think it's necessary for you to see the body. You've identified these things as belonging to him." Russ wanted to get her out of there. He couldn't stand the tears, wanted to see her eyes flash with fire, the amused arch of an eyebrow, that naughty grin.

She gave him back the wallet and the ring and sagged against the wall once again. Closing her eyes for a moment, she let her shoulders droop with sorrow. She felt so vulnerable. But it lasted only a moment. Straightening, she looked at him once again, this time the tears gone, replaced by an implacable strength. "I have to do it. I have to see him. Otherwise it won't be real."

Russ nodded. Placing an arm around her, he opened the door and led her into the room. He tightened his embrace as they got closer. Taking a deep breath, he removed the sheet, exposing the face of the dead man.

Bonnie gasped and hid her face against Russ's chest. With an emotional oath, Russ pulled the sheet back up and pulled her out of the room.

She was crying now, her sobs soft, but deep. "Shhh," Russ whispered, stroking her hair, rubbing her back, wishing he could take the pain away from her. "I'm sorry, Bonnie. I'm so sorry."

She shook her head, a burst of laughter escaping through the sobs. She's hysterical, he thought, his heart aching for her. He tightened his arms around her as if he could shield her from the heartache.

"Russ—oh, God." She struggled away from him, freeing herself and staring at him. "Oh, Russ, that's not my brother."

He stared at her, unable to comprehend what she was telling him. "Bonnie, what are you talking about?"

"That man in there. I don't know who he is, but he's not Sam."

Chapter Seven

"Russ, I'm telling you—that man in there is not my brother," Bonnie repeated.

"But the ring...the wallet?" Russ stared at her in bewilderment.

"I don't know how he got Sam's things. I can't explain any of it." She grabbed Russ's arm and tugged him toward the stairs. "Come on, let's get out of here. We've got to tell Carolyn."

When they got back outside, Bonnie threw her arms around Russ's neck. "Oh, Russ, I feel like singing and dancing." The happiness on her face faded and she bit her bottom lip. "It's horrible to be happy. I mean, that man is somebody's son, maybe somebody's husband. You must think I'm awful to feel so relieved."

Russ smiled at her and ran his fingertip down the side of her face. "You aren't awful. You're human." He cupped her chin, wanting to capture the softness of her features, this moment when her defenses were down and vulnerability shone in her eyes.

Without thought, he bent his head and touched her lips gently, softly, with his own. He ended the kiss immediately and drew back, saw the confusion in her eyes and felt an echo of the same emotion inside himself. "Come on, let's go tell Carolyn and Beau," he said.

They rode back to the house in silence. Russ glanced at Bonnie again and again, seeing the exhaustion mixed with relief on her face. She leaned against the passenger-side door, as if too tired to sit up straight. He knew she was feeling the aftermath of the emotional roller coaster of the past hour. "You okay?" he finally asked, needing to break the silence, connect with her in some way.

She nodded. "Just thinking."

She shifted positions, leaned closer to him as if needing the same thing he did...a connection with somebody warm and alive.

"I'm so glad it wasn't Sam, but that puts us right back where we started. Where is Sam, and why in God's name doesn't he contact one of us? Why hasn't he turned himself in to the police and tried to prove his innocence in Father's murder?" She rubbed her forehead, as if the questions were simply too much to handle.

Russ reached out and touched her hand with his. "I wish I had the answers for you. So far Beau hasn't come up with any answers, either."

"I wish I knew how that man got Sam's wallet and his wedding ring. Sam never took that ring off."

Her hand curled, her fingers entwining with his, and he knew she was afraid that Sam hadn't given up the wedding band voluntarily.

He gently squeezed her hand. "Perhaps we'll have some answers when we get an ID on the dead man."

She nodded and was quiet. She didn't relinquish her hold on his hand, nor did Russ break the contact. It wasn't until he pulled into the Randolf driveway and parked behind Beau's car that he finally released her hand to shut off the engine.

"Russ, thank you for being here for me."

Her gaze lingered on him, again a touch of confusion darkening their blue depths. He wondered what was going on in that crazy head of hers. He wondered why he cared.

As they got out of the car, the warm night air surrounded them. Russ could smell the flowers in the front yard, and beneath it the subtle scent of Bonnie's perfume. The scent tightened his stomach muscles, reminded him of the sweet pleasure of kissing her, a pleasure he wanted to repeat.

Only this time he knew it wasn't just lust driving him. He wanted to kiss her until the sadness in her eyes was gone; longed to hold her until her naughty smile was back, taunting him with wicked pleasure. He wanted her irreverence and mocking arrogance.

She hesitated at the doorway, as if sensing his desire. When she tilted her head to look up at him, the moonlight found and loved her face, making her features more lovely than ever.

"Russ? You know the other night when you said something powerful was at work between us?"

"Yes?" He couldn't resist. Reaching up a fingertip, he smoothed a strand of her dark hair away from her eyes.

"I just wanted to tell you you're right." Without waiting for his reply, she turned and disappeared into the house, leaving him to stand on the porch, still smelling her perfume and wanting her more than ever.

Ribs sizzled as they cooked, filling the air with their delicious scent. "Those smell wonderful!" Bonnie exclaimed to Waylon, who stood in front of the barbecue pit, standing guard over the ribs like a mother pit bull over her puppies.

"It's my secret recipe," the chubby deputy exclaimed. "Passed down to me from generations of finger-lickin' rib cookers."

"I can't wait to taste them," Bonnie replied, her gaze roving over the backyard. Everywhere she looked there was activity. Waylon's kids played with the twins in a plastic-turtle sandbox, their laughter riding on the warm breeze. Carolyn, Brenda Jo and Waylon's wife, Regina, all made trips back and forth from the kitchen to the picnic table in the backyard, their hands laden with food. The rest of the men, Beau, Lloyd and Russ, sat in lawn chairs, drinking beer and telling tales, their laughter competing with the noise from the kids.

The only one alone was Daniel. He sat on a lawn chair, watching the other kids play but refusing to take part in the fun. As usual, a scowl decorated his face, detracting from his little-boy handsomeness.

Bonnie frowned, her gaze drifting back to Russ. He was as handsome as sin. Wearing worn, tight jeans and a navy blue T-shirt, he was relaxed and smiling as he listened to whatever Beau was saying.

Since the night they'd gone to identify the body a week earlier, Bonnie had fought confusion about her feelings for Russ. Despite her resolve to the contrary, she was beginning to care for him...too much. It scared her, and for the past week she had consciously remained aloof from him.

"Hand me that jar of sauce, would you, darlin'?" Waylon's question pulled her from her thoughts. She grabbed the jar of red sauce and handed it to him. "So, you liking Casey's Corners all right?" Waylon asked, brushing the ribs with his secret concoction.

"Sure, it's a terrific little town," Bonnie answered, grateful to have something to take her mind off her warring emotions where Russ was concerned.

"We're a little town that's growing by leaps and bounds. People are looking for good places to raise families, and Casey's Corners is one of the best." He shot her a sideways glance. "People like Russ."

Bonnie looked back over to where Daniel still sat alone. "I have a feeling it's going to take more than Casey's Corners to raise that kid."

Waylon nodded. "That's one sad little boy."

"Sad?" Bonnie laughed in protest. "He's got a lot of rage, but I don't think he's sad. What he needs is for Russ to lay down the law."

"Russ knows what he's doing with his son."

But Bonnie wasn't so sure. Twice in the past week Russ had had to leave work to deal with problems with Daniel. The kid was a delinquent in the making, and Russ didn't seem to be taking any steps to stop it.

It's not my problem, she told herself. Russ would be dealing with Daniel long after she left Casey's Corners. She was surprised to realize that the thought of leaving the little town was vaguely depressing.

Another couple of weeks and she'd have her quarterly inheritance check, then she could decide what she wanted to do. Today nothing should be on her mind except enjoying the company of her friends and family.

She drifted into the kitchen, where the women sat at the table, drinking tall glasses of iced tea. "Hmm, that looks good," she said.

Regina smiled. "Nothing is better than drinking a glass of iced tea inside with all the kids outside."

They laughed, and Bonnie poured herself a glass and sat down across from her sister. "Can I do anything to help? When I came in those ribs smelled about ready to eat."

Carolyn shook her head. "Everything is done. We're just enjoying a moment of peace before we head back out to feed the kids."

Regina eyed Bonnie, then Brenda Jo. "Believe me, one day you two will know how precious the time is when you have a moment to yourself without somebody yelling 'Mommy.'"

"Not me," Brenda Jo said, her voice heavy with sadness. "My biological clock has already stopped ticking." She leaned over and covered Bonnie's hand with hers. "Don't you make the same mistake, hon. Don't party and play until one day you wake up and realize you've wasted the best years of your life."

Bonnie laughed self-consciously. "Goodness, I'm only twenty-five. I've got lots of time left before my biological clock runs down."

Brenda Jo shook her head with a wistful smile. "Just remember what I said. It's amazing how quickly life goes by, especially when you think you're having fun."

Brenda Jo's words haunted Bonnie throughout the afternoon. "When you think you're having fun." Bonnie's adult life had been filled with fun, but there had been plenty of deeply lonely nights, too. Everybody loved a party girl, but when the party was over, Bonnie was always alone.

The night Russ had taken her to identify the body, Bonnie had been grateful for his quiet strength, the support she knew he offered her. It had been nice to lean on somebody strong, nice not to be alone.

She looked across the picnic table, where Russ sat next to Daniel. Russ was leaning down, whispering in Daniel's ear. As if he felt her gaze, Russ raised his eyes to her, his lips curving up in the teasing smile she'd come to anticipate.

"Bonnie, Daniel was just telling me he saw a sign saying a carnival would be in town next weekend. We thought we might go Saturday night. Want to come?"

"Is this a date?" she asked automatically, expecting their usual banter.

He tilted his head and gazed at her for a long moment, the cocoa color of his eyes warmer than she'd ever seen them.

"Yeah," he finally answered. "Yeah, it is a date."

Surprise rippled through her at his unexpected response. What was he doing? Why wasn't he playing the game? "Sure, okay," she finally replied, her face warming as she realized everyone at the table was watching them.

"Who is ready for birthday cake?" Carolyn asked, and was answered by a chorus of moans.

"If I eat another bite I'll bust!" Lloyd exclaimed, and they all echoed his sentiment.

Beau leaned back, a satisfied smile on his face. "Nothing like good food and good company to make a man's birthday almost perfect."

"Almost perfect?" Carolyn eyed him in mock indignation. "What else could I do to make it more perfect?"

He leaned over and whispered something in her ear. Her face blushed bright pink and she slapped him playfully on the arm as everyone laughed. Bonnie didn't miss the look of pure love between her sister and Beau, and again she felt a longing deep inside her.

She stood up and busied herself clearing off the table. Regina and Brenda Jo helped while Carolyn put the twins down for a nap. The phone rang and Beau excused himself to answer it.

Carolyn had just come out of the twins' room and Bonnie stood at the sink scrapping dishes, when Beau emerged from the bedroom where he had taken the phone call. "That was Dave from the station. We finally got an ID on our John Doe."

"Who?" Bonnie asked as Russ came in the back door and stood just behind her.

"His name is Richard Burwell from Wichita. He has a rap sheet a mile long—breaking and entering, pickpocketing, petty theft. If I was to guess, I'd say he probably stole that stuff from Sam." Beau frowned. "Of course, that doesn't tell us anything about who killed Richard Burwell or where Sam might be now." He placed an arm around Carolyn. "I don't know, honey, but dead bodies seem to appear around your brother."

"You can't think that Sam killed that man," Bonnie protested. "That doesn't even make sense."

"No, I don't think that," Beau assured her. "Surely Sam would be smart enough to remove his own identification."

Bonnie frowned thoughtfully. "What scares me is the thought that Richard Burwell was killed because he had Sam's identification."

Everyone was silent for a moment as Bonnie's words sank in. "That falls in with the belief I've had all along," Carolyn finally said, her voice heavy with worry. "I think somebody is after Sam. He's in danger, and that's why he hasn't contacted any of us." Carolyn turned into Beau's arms and rested her head on his shoulder.

Russ reached out and touched Bonnie's arm. "We've all decided to take the kids down to the park for a game of softball. Want to come?"

"Okay," she agreed. Maybe it would be best to give Carolyn and Beau a little time alone.

Minutes later, a noisy group walked the block and a half to the small park. Waylon and Regina's four kids ran ahead of the adults, and Daniel lagged behind, dragging his feet and mumbling.

"Daniel doesn't seem to be having a very good time," Bonnie said to Russ, who walked beside her.

"Daniel is testing me."

"Testing you?" Bonnie eyed Russ curiously, not understanding. "What do you mean?"

"It's kind of hard to explain. Daniel was never real close to Anne, but when she left, it really shook him up. Daniel is testing me to see if my love for him is unconditional."

"Is it?"

He looked at her in surprise. "Of course it is. Believe me, Bonnie. When I love, I love unconditionally."

"Come on, you dawdlers," Waylon shouted moments later from the center of the baseball diamond. "Let's pick some teams and play ball."

The rest of the afternoon whizzed by. The ball game was the wildest, craziest Bonnie had ever played. Waylon and Russ made up the rules as they went, and most plays dissolved into helpless laughter as the two deputies argued each and every call Regina made as official umpire. Even Daniel, for most of the afternoon, transformed into a normal, heathy boy enjoying a game of ball.

It was nearly dark when they decided to call it a day. Regina and Waylon gathered their brood and took off toward their home several blocks away, and Russ and

Daniel walked with Bonnie back to Beau and Carolyn's house.

"This has been fun," Bonnie said, not eager to get back to the house and have the day end.

"Yeah, this is the kind of stuff I wanted when I chose Casey's Corners as our new home. I interviewed in half a dozen small towns, but none of them compared."

"Did you have fun today, Daniel?" Bonnie turned and asked the boy, who lagged behind them.

He shrugged. "It was okay."

Bonnie felt an edge of frustration. She'd tried all afternoon to crack Daniel's tough-guy exterior, but he was unrelenting. She still didn't think Russ had a handle on the situation with Daniel. It's not my problem, she reminded herself. Russ would handle his son the best way he knew how, and Bonnie had nothing to do with it.

"It feels a little bit cooler tonight," she said, changing the subject.

"Hmm, autumn is just around the corner."

Russ grinned at her, and in the falling shadows, she saw the sparkle in his eyes.

"Autumn is my favorite time of year." He moved closer to her, his shoulder brushing against her as they walked. "Crisp, cool nights...cuddling under a warm blanket, the sound of rain on the roof." His voice was low, as soft as a caress. "Autumn is lovers' weather."

She looked at him in surprise, her heart suddenly stepping up its rhythm. "Be careful, Russ. You're beginning to sound like a boxers kind of man."

They paused in front of Beau and Carolyn's house. "I think you're a very bad influence on me, Bonnie Baker. You have me thinking wild and crazy thoughts."

Bonnie was vaguely aware of Daniel continuing down the sidewalk. Her mouth was unaccountably dry as she gazed at Russ in expectation. "What kind of wild and crazy thoughts?"

He stepped closer to her, so close the tips of her breasts pressed against his muscular chest. "You have me wondering what kind of little sounds you would make if I kissed your ear, nibbled on the lobe. You've got me wondering what you look like first thing in the morning after a night of lovemaking."

Bonnie gasped, her heart thumping so rapidly, she was certain it would explode right out of her chest. He touched her mouth with the tip of his index finger.

"Oh, yes, Bonnie...if one of these days I end up running down Main Street in a pair of boxers, you'll know it's all because of you."

Bonnie stepped back from him, unsure if she wanted the distance or wanted him to do all the things he'd told her he wondered about.

"Dad, come on," Daniel said, his voice filled with impatience.

"I'm coming, Daniel," Russ answered, then looked back at Bonnie. "Good night, Princess."

He cupped her chin with his fingers, his eyes filled with a white heat that threatened to melt Bonnie into a puddle.

"Sweet dreams." He released her, then turned and headed down the sidewalk, where his son awaited him.

Bonnie stared after him. For the first time she hadn't minded him calling her "Princess," and she knew it was because this time when he'd said it his tone had been different. He'd said it as a caress, the same way he might have said "sweetheart" or "darling."

She was in trouble. Deep trouble. She didn't know when it had happened, couldn't explain how it had happened. But somehow, someway, she had fallen in love with Russ.

Chapter Eight

"Garrison, I'm at Carolyn's home in Casey's Corners. Please call me here. I need to talk to you." Bonnie slammed down the phone. Whoever had invented voice mail should be shot. This was the third message she'd left for Garrison in as many days, and she had yet to hear back from her late father's business partner.

"He probably knows why I'm calling, and that's why he's avoiding me," she mumbled as she flopped down on the sofa in the living room. Around her the house was silent. Too silent. Beau and Carolyn had left with the twins earlier, having planned an evening of cards with Waylon and Regina. They'd invited Bonnie to go along, but she had declined, knowing she was too cranky and out of sorts to inflict her company on anyone.

Why didn't Garrison call her back? She intended to press him for her money, hoping he could get her a check soon. Ever since the night of the barbecue, the night she realized she had fallen in love with Russ Blackburn, she'd battled the need to get out of town, run as far and as fast as possible. How fast did you have to move to outrun heartache? she wondered.

She certainly had no illusions about any kind of a future with Russ. He wanted her. Certainly he'd shown his desire for her. But he hadn't pretended to be in love with her. Heck, half the time he didn't even pretend to like her very much.

How long could she remain here in town, continue to play little games with Russ that merely stoked the sexual tension between them, without an explosion eventually? And certainly an explosion would only lead to one conclusion: they would fall into bed and make love.

She got off the sofa, restless energy forcing her to pace the room as she tried to rid herself of thoughts of Russ. She looked at her watch and frowned. It was only a few minutes after eight o'clock. It would still be a couple of hours before Carolyn and Beau got home.

The house was so quiet, but Bonnie was reluctant to turn on the television. Instead she opted for the stereo, finding several cassettes of country music to play. As the robust sounds of Garth Brooks filled the house, Bonnie went into Carolyn and Beau's bedroom.

Opening the closet door, she immediately spied her wedding dress hanging beneath a clear plastic wrap. Reaching out, she touched the plastic gently. She didn't regret running out on Helmut. Although she had been fond of the handsome prince, her feelings for him didn't come close to what she felt for Russ. She hadn't loved Helmut. The only thing she truly regretted was losing perhaps her only opportunity to be a bride.

On impulse, she took the gown from the closet, removed the plastic protection, then laid the garment on the bed. After undressing, she pulled the gown on over her head, allowing the silken folds to fall to the floor. She fastened the tiny, pearl, seed buttons, then stared at her reflection in the dresser mirror.

She had to admit—she would have made an attractive bride. Funny that she had picked a very traditional gown, when she'd spent much of her life proving to people how untraditional she could be.

Closing her eyes, for a moment she imagined herself walking down a flower-bedecked church aisle. At the end of the aisle, standing tall and proud, was Russ, sinfully handsome in a black tuxedo. It was a beautiful picture, one that made her heart expand with warmth and her mouth grow dry with longing.

She left the bedroom and went into the kitchen. Pouring herself a glass of iced tea from the refrigerator, she once again felt the stir of old dreams, dreams she knew in her heart would never be realized.

She sat down at the table, knowing she could fantasize all she wanted about a wedding with Russ, but it would forever remain just a wistful fantasy.

When he chose his wife, the woman who would be a stepmother to Daniel, it wouldn't be someone who'd been arrested for swimming in a fountain in Paris. It wouldn't be someone who'd run out on a prince.

Russ would pick a woman who could cook, who could dry dishes without getting her hand stuck in a glass. He'd want a woman who wasn't impulsive and frivolous. He deserved the kind of woman Bonnie never would be, never could be. Daniel deserved the kind of mother Bonnie had dreamed of having when she was a child, one who would know and understand a little boy's needs.

She fingered the lace that trimmed the bodice of her gown, wishing she could be different. But, she knew the kind of person she was, had heard it said all her life. No matter how hard she'd tried, her father had deemed her unacceptable. She'd learned to live with that particular pain, but she couldn't stand it if Russ was disappointed in her. And eventually, if they spent enough time together, he'd know her father had been right. She was worthless. Better to run. It had always been better to run.

The country music that had surrounded her stopped, the tape finished. Bonnie frowned as she

heard a faint sound coming from one of the bedrooms. It had sounded like the creak of a floorboard.

She stood up, cursing the rustling of the gown she
wore. She strained, body tense as she tried to listen
over the sudden, frantic beating of her heart. Again
she heard it—this time the distinct sound of a furtive
footstep against a hardwood floor. Panic swirled
through her. Somebody was in the house with her.
Somebody who shouldn't be.

Frozen, she tried to think of what to do. Unwilling
to confront whoever might be present, she finally
moved as quietly as she could to the telephone. Picking up the receiver, she punched in the seven numbers
to the police station. She nearly sobbed in relief when
Russ answered the phone.

"Russ...somebody's in the house," she whispered.

"Bonnie, is that you?"

She stifled the impulse to scream. "Yes, it's me.
Beau and Carolyn are gone, but somebody is in one of
the bedrooms. I heard something...a noise coming
from in there."

"Maybe it's a mouse. Sit tight. I'll be right over."
He hung up and Bonnie did the same.

Was it possible that what she'd heard was a mouse
in the house? If that was the case and Russ showed up,
she'd feel like a complete fool.

Going to a kitchen drawer, she carefully withdrew
a butcher knife. She knew she would never be able to

use it against anybody, but she felt better with it in her hand.

Sticking her head out the kitchen doorway, she peered down the hallway. She thought she heard a faint rattling, but didn't trust that it wasn't her imagination working overtime. A mouse?

"Hello?" she yelled. "Is somebody there?"

A moment of silence followed, then she heard footsteps moving quickly across the floor. Then nothing. If it was a mouse, it was a rodent with very big feet.

"Bonnie?"

She nearly sobbed in relief at the sound of Russ at the front door. "Somebody is in the bedroom, and it isn't a mouse," she said as she let him in.

"Put that knife away before you hurt yourself," Russ commanded as he drew his gun. "And wait here." He disappeared down the hallway. Bonnie's heart pounded erratically as she waited, still clutching the knife.

"Bonnie, it's okay," he called from her bedroom.

She hurried in, surprised to see the screen missing from her window and her jewelry box dumped out in the middle of her bed.

"You were right—somebody was here. But not any longer."

His gaze swept her from head to toe, and she suddenly remembered the wedding gown.

"Planning a wedding?" he asked.

She flushed with embarrassment. "I was just trying it on, wasting some time..." She allowed her voice to trail off. "What are you doing standing there staring at me?" she demanded, grabbing onto anger to hide her embarrassment. "Why don't you go after whoever was in here sorting through my jewelry box?"

"Why don't you look through your things and see if anything was stolen? I'll go check to see if anything was disturbed elsewhere." He strode out of her bedroom and into Carolyn and Beau's room, where he drew in a deep breath, trying to forget how beautiful Bonnie had looked in the bridal gown.

He shook his head and shoved thoughts of Bonnie away as he surveyed the bedroom. As with Bonnie's room, nothing appeared to have been disturbed except the wooden jewelry box on top of the dresser. The contents were strewn all over, as if somebody had been searching for something specific.

"They were in here, too." Bonnie stated the obvious as she stepped into the bedroom, her gaze focused on the scattered jewelry. "My necklace is missing. The one my father gave me."

Russ frowned, trying to keep his thoughts on what she was saying, not how she looked. All that frothy lace, and those tiny buttons that just begged to be unfastened.

"Was it an expensive necklace?" he finally asked.

She shrugged. "Not particularly. It was a gold charm of a phoenix." She moved over to the dresser and searched through Carolyn's things. "I don't see Caro's here, either. It was exactly like mine." She frowned. "Why would anyone sneak into the house and steal those necklaces and nothing else? I have a diamond tennis bracelet and a pair of diamond earrings, but they weren't stolen."

Russ ran a hand through his hair, finding it difficult to think, to breathe, whenever he looked at her. "I'm going to go outside and look around. I'll be back in just a few minutes."

Once outside, he did a cursory check of the property, although he already knew the point of entry was Bonnie's bedroom window and that whoever had been in there was long gone. Why would somebody break into a house for a gold necklace and leave more valuable jewelry behind? It made no sense. Nor did it make sense for his stomach to clench and his groin to tighten just because Bonnie had looked so gorgeous in a wedding dress.

He frowned, taking another few minutes to inspect the Randolf property. Discovering nothing amiss, he went back inside, relieved to find that Bonnie had changed into slacks and a blouse and he smelled fresh-brewed coffee.

"Did you find anything?" she asked as she led him into the kitchen.

"Nothing, but I really didn't expect to." He sank down at the table, nodding when she held up a cup. "Whoever was in here was a professional."

"A professional? What do you mean?" She poured them each coffee and joined him at the table.

Russ rubbed his forehead thoughtfully. "Nobody but a professional thief or a complete idiot would risk entering a house with somebody home."

Bonnie's eyes were filled with confusion. "Maybe it was just an idiot?"

Russ shook his head. "Whoever it was, he knew exactly what he wanted. He got in and out in a matter of minutes." He grinned. "An idiot definitely would have gone for the glittering stuff...like diamonds."

"But why would anyone want to steal those necklaces?" Bonnie asked.

"I don't know. You tell me."

She shrugged and stared down into her coffee cup. Again Russ's heart stepped up its rhythm as he studied her features. He wished he could figure out exactly what it was about her that so captivated him.

"You've been avoiding me at work all week," he finally remarked.

"I've had a lot on my mind." Still she didn't look at him.

As always when she was quiet, introspective, he wished he could crawl inside her, read her thoughts, understand the workings of her crazy, impulsive mind. "Like what?"

Finally she looked up, her blue eyes sparkling with the bravado he'd come to anticipate.

"Like where I want to go when I get my next inheritance check and leave Casey's Corners."

Russ felt as if he'd been sucker punched. Her words shouldn't have affected him. He'd always known she'd leave. That's what women like Bonnie did. Still, he hadn't expected the gnawing hollowness in the pit of his stomach when he contemplated her absence from his life.

He drained his coffee cup and stood up. "I have total confidence that your new destination will be wonderfully exciting and sinfully expensive."

Her eyes glittered overbright. "Is there a better way to live?"

He shook his head, his gaze lingering on her. "Not for a princess." She got up and walked with him to the front door. "When are you expecting to leave?"

She shrugged. "I don't know. I've been trying to get hold of Garrison to see if he'll cut my check a little early."

"Surely you won't leave before Saturday. You know we have a date for the carnival. Daniel would be disappointed if you couldn't come."

"I certainly wouldn't want to disappoint Daniel. Besides, Garrison is a stickler for rules. He'll probably make me wait until the check is supposed to be released."

Russ knew he should leave, knew he should get the hell away from her before he did something stupid. But even though the front door was only inches away, he couldn't make himself move toward it. Instead he closed the distance between Bonnie and him, wanting to kiss her, needing to taste the sweetness of her lips just once more.

He didn't give her time to protest, didn't want to give himself a chance to reconsider. Without pause he wrapped her in his arms and captured her mouth with his.

She hesitated only a moment before responding, then her hands reached up around his neck and her body melted against his. Her mouth was sweet heat, infusing him with a heady desire that made thinking impossible.

There was no sense of growing desire. The moment their lips met Russ was fully aroused. It was instantaneous, and he allowed the sensations of kissing Bonnie, smelling Bonnie, holding Bonnie to carry him away from sanity.

With his lips still on hers, he guided her over to the sofa, where they sank down, still entwined in each other's arms.

All thought of time and place left Russ as he fell into the enchantment of Bonnie. Her scent surrounded him, the mysterious, spicy perfume that had haunted him from the moment he'd first met her.

He moved his lips from her mouth to her ear, nibbling on the lobe as she moaned. Never had he wanted a woman the way he wanted her. Never in his life had he felt such overwhelming desire to possess, consume, love a woman.

"Bonnie, sweet Bonnie," he whispered against the smooth hollow of her neck. Her hands tangled in his hair, pulling his mouth back to hers.

She arched against him, the heat of her body radiating through their clothes, as if she were on the verge of combustion. And that's exactly how Russ felt, as if he were on the verge of bursting into flames. He moved his hands beneath her blouse, stroking the silky skin of her back, loving the throaty sounds she made with each caress.

His breaths were ragged, alien to his ears, but there was harmony in the fact that Bonnie's breathing matched his, and he knew she was as much a prisoner of desire as he. His fingers lingered over the clasp of her bra, and when she didn't protest, he undid it. As he moved his hands around to cup her breasts, her moan of pleasure almost snapped what little control he retained.

He shifted their position so she was beneath him and he could see her face as he stroked the hardened peaks of her breasts. Oh, God, she was so beautiful. Her cheeks were flushed, her eyes half-closed but glazed with fire. Torn between the desire to rip off her clothes and make love fast and furious, or take his time and savor each and every caress, each and every moan, he struggled to go slow, to relish this moment of madness.

He raised up, removing his hands from her breasts, instead fumbling with the buttons on her blouse, wanting her naked in his arms. Cursing inwardly, he worked clumsily, taking an eternity to unfasten the first button.

She smiled, an alluring smile that sent his blood pounding through his veins. Pushing his hand away, she unbuttoned the blouse and shrugged out of it, taking off her bra, as well.

For a moment Russ stared at her, awed by her perfection, humbled by her sharing it with him. "Bonnie, you are so beautiful," he whispered. He bent his head and touched the tip of his tongue to a turgid nipple, reveling in her gasp of pleasure. His tongue lathed first one, then the other peak, loving the taste of her, the feel of her arching up to press intimately against him.

"Bonnie, I want you," he murmured urgently. "Oh, Princess, I want to make love to you."

She released a tremulous sigh and her eyes were suddenly filled with confusion. "Russ...I don't...I can't..." She pressed gently against his chest.

He stared down at her, disappointment expanding where desire had been. He knew he could have her. Her protest had been feeble and she watched him expectantly, as if uncertain what she wanted, what she needed.

But he didn't want her this way. When he made love to Bonnie he wanted her to want him completely, without hesitation, without reluctance. "You're right. Get dressed, Bonnie," he said, rising to stand next to where she remained on the sofa.

She sat up and grabbed her blouse, quickly pulling it on, her gaze not meeting his. "I'm sorry, Russ."

He wanted to be angry with her, would welcome the clean, uncomplicated emotion of wrath. But she looked as miserable as he felt, and he simply couldn't be angry with her. "If the time isn't right, it's not right," he said softly.

He didn't want to think that this might be the one and only chance he could have to make love to her. He didn't want to consider that she might leave tomorrow, and always remain a piece of unfinished business in his life.

"I've got to get back to the station," he said once she was dressed again. "I'll write up a report and talk to Beau later about the break-in." He moved to the door, still fighting the desire to complete what they had begun.

"Will I ever get my necklace back?" she asked, obviously attempting to diffuse the tension between them.

"I wouldn't count on it. I'll send a description to the area pawnshops, but I really don't expect it to turn up there. If whoever took it was looking for something to turn into quick cash, he would have taken your diamonds."

She nodded and stood up, her face still a study in bewilderment and, oddly, pain. "Russ...I... Oh, never mind."

"I'll talk to you later." He turned and left the house, confusion muddying his thoughts. As he drove back to the station, he tried to sort through the myriad emotions that coursed through him.

Disappointment, that was an easy one to identify. Even now his body ached with unfulfillment. He'd wanted Bonnie...badly. She'd taken him to the peak of excitement, then left him hanging without finishing what they'd begun.

Yet he couldn't summon any anger. She hadn't been teasing him; calling a halt to their lovemaking had been difficult for her. And probably it had been wise.

She was leaving town, perhaps within days. Unfortunately he had a feeling this wouldn't be a case of out of sight, out of mind. He parked his car and shut off the engine. Instead of getting out, he remained, his hands clenched on the steering wheel.

Making love to Bonnie would have been a major mistake, one he feared would have scarred his heart forever. When had his heart become involved?

He leaned his head back and closed his eyes, for a moment remembering the way Bonnie had looked in that damned wedding gown. She'd been beautiful, a stunning vision in satin and lace...and he'd wanted her to be his bride.

Pain stirred in his chest. He'd always believed that when he fell in love again, he'd be happy and know he'd found the missing link in his life.

He got out of the car and walked toward the station, feeling more alone than he could ever remember as he realized he was in love. Too bad he'd been stupid enough to fall in love with a woman who would soon be missing from his life.

Chapter Nine

"Are you sure you feel like going with Russ and Daniel this morning?" Carolyn asked Bonnie worriedly.

Bonnie nodded. "Yeah, I'm all right, just tired." She rubbed her forehead. "I've been having bad dreams lately."

Carolyn joined her at the table, the twins content for a moment in their high chairs with a handful of raisins and a piece of toast in front of them. "I know what you mean. I've had a few myself. I still can't believe somebody was in our house, going through our things." She frowned thoughtfully. "I just can't imagine why somebody wanted our necklaces."

"Neither can I, but that's not what I've been dreaming about." Bonnie paused a moment to sip her orange juice.

"What's up?" Carolyn said. She reached over and covered one of Bonnie's hands. "Come on, Bonnie, it usually helps to talk about nightmares."

Bonnie sighed, wishing she'd never brought up the subject.

"Bonnie, tell me," Carolyn prodded again.

"At first, they were all about Sam," she began reluctantly. She described her recurring dream in detail. Carolyn nodded, encouraging her to continue. "Anyway, I had that dream over and over again, then in the past couple of nights it changed."

"To what?"

Bonnie sighed, thinking of the dream that had awakened her the past several mornings. "Now I'm running down a highway, and I know something horrible is chasing me. I run so fast my side aches, my legs burn and my heart feels like it's going to explode. But I know if I stop or slow down, whatever is behind me will catch me."

Bonnie tightened her fingers around the glass of juice. "But then I'm exhausted and can't run anymore. I finally stop, and when I turn around, nothing is behind me. Nothing is chasing me." She laughed self-consciously. "I know it sounds stupid, but every morning I wake up scared because I don't know what's making me run.''

Carolyn released her hand and shrugged. ''Honey, dreams sometimes just don't make any sense.'' She jumped up as Brent began throwing his raisins on the floor. ''Try to put it all behind you and have a good time at the carnival. It's going to be a gorgeous day.''

Bonnie summoned a smile, although she wasn't looking forward to the outing at all. In fact, she dreaded it. How was she ever going to make it through the day without falling more deeply in love with Russ? She still couldn't believe how close she had come to throwing her heart to the Fates and making love to him the other night.

''Speaking of the carnival, what time are Russ and Daniel picking you up?'' Carolyn asked.

''Ten.'' Bonnie looked at the clock on the oven and jumped up in surprise. ''I'd better get moving—that only gives me about twenty-five minutes to pull myself together.''

A few minutes later she stood beneath the shower, her thoughts once again consumed with Russ. Things had been awkward between them at work since the night they had almost made love. Russ had been distant, and for the first time in her life, Bonnie hadn't known how to act.

She'd finally heard from Garrison, and he'd agreed to get her the check within the coming week. So she was mere days away from leaving Casey's Corners, walking away from the friends she made and the man she loved.

It can be no other way, she told herself as the spray from the shower washed away her shampoo. I'm not right for Russ. I'll never be the right woman for him. She had spent her life disappointing the people closest to her. She simply couldn't live knowing she'd disappointed Russ. Wiping at her eyes, she wasn't sure they stung because of the shampoo or because of her thoughts.

By the time she had dressed, she had decided to accept the day with Russ and Daniel as a gift to herself. She wouldn't think about leaving, she wouldn't think about how painful her heartache would be. She would simply enjoy a day spent with the man she loved...and his demon child. She smiled sadly at this thought.

Yes, as far as she was concerned, Daniel was the child from hell. Rebellious, stubborn, defiant—funny how he reminded her of herself. He was lucky to have Russ. Russ would eventually marry a woman who would head the PTA, bake cookies for school parties, a traditional woman with traditional values. He was a briefs man, totally wrong for Bonnie.

"Bonnie, Russ and Daniel are here," Carolyn called from the living room.

Bonnie stared at her reflection a final time. "Seize the day...and to hell with tomorrow," she said to the woman in the mirror. Besides—she raised her chin defiantly—there were places to go, adventures to be had, she'd never be happy in this little one-horse town. She turned away from the mirror, before she could see the untruth of her thoughts radiating from her eyes.

"Hi, guys," she greeted Russ and Daniel as she walked into the living room. She tried not to notice how achingly handsome Russ looked in his tight, worn blue jeans and the neatly ironed, short-sleeved sport shirt. However, she couldn't help but notice the scowl on Daniel's face. "You ready to go on all the rides and eat cotton candy until you throw up?"

"Gee, that sounds like fun," Russ said dryly.

Bonnie ignored him, pleased when a ghost of a smile danced at the corners of Daniel's mouth. It was there only a moment, then gone, but still it warmed Bonnie's heart.

"Ah, come on, Russ. A carnival isn't fun unless you're a little more than half-sick by the end of the day," she replied.

Russ shot Carolyn a long-suffering look. "I think I'm in for a day to remember," he declared.

Carolyn laughed. "Beau said that if he can get a couple of hours off we might hit the carnival. Maybe we'll see you there," she said as she walked with them to the front door.

"Great, the more the merrier," Bonnie replied.

A day to remember. Bonnie knew that was what the day would be. A day of memories for her to take with her wherever she went when she left Casey's Corners.

"A penny for your thoughts," Russ said as they got into the car.

His words pulled her from her momentary reverie, and she grinned at him. "Like I'd tell you for a mere penny," she quipped.

He returned her grin with one of his own. "Like they're worth more than a penny."

She laughed, glad they were back to normal, the strain of the past couple of days gone. He started the car with a roar and they headed toward the field on the north side of town where the carnival had put down roots for the next two weeks.

As he drove, they talked of inconsequential things—the approaching end of summer, the work he was doing on his house, the new family who had moved in down the street from Carolyn and Beau. Small talk that was nonthreatening; light talk that was pleasant in its lack of importance.

When the carnival came into view, both Daniel and Bonnie sat up straighter in their seats. A wave of anticipation swept through Bonnie. She loved carnivals, and despite the neutral look on Daniel's face, she could see his excitement shining in his eyes. "Wow, look at all the rides!" she exclaimed. "I see a Tilt-a-whirl and an octopus ride, and look, there's one of those barrels you stand in and they whirl around, then the bottom drops out.''

''The bottom drops out?''

Daniel had uttered his first words since they'd picked her up.

''Yeah, it spins so fast the centrifugal force plasters you against the wall, then the bottom falls out and you just hang there, stuck to the wall,'' she explained. ''It's one of my favorites.''

For a moment Daniel's face reflected awe, then he frowned. ''Sounds stupid.''

The little scamp, Bonnie thought, turning back around to face out the front window. If she needed any other support that she was absolutely wrong for Russ, she didn't have to look any further. The kid hated her... and she wasn't real fond of him, either.

''Personally, the Ferris wheel is my favorite,'' Russ said as he parked the car. ''I love being up so high, gazing out over the countryside, seeing the people and the cars on the ground looking so small.''

''Not me,'' Bonnie declared. ''I love speed, but I don't love heights.''

''I'd like to get out of here,'' Daniel said impatiently from the back seat.

Russ and Bonnie laughed. ''It's a deal, sport,'' Russ said, and the three of them tumbled out of the car.

Bonnie breathed deeply of the air rich with the smells of a carnival. The scents of warm, roasted peanuts, sweet cotton candy and hot pretzels all mingled with the fragrant summer day.

A day of memories. As the day progressed, Bonnie clutched each and every moment to her heart to savor when she was alone in some faraway place with people who meant nothing to her. When they rode the bumper cars, she captured the sound of Russ's devilish laughter each time he managed to collide into her car. As they enjoyed the Tilt-a-whirl, she cherished the feel of his broad shoulders, the warmth of his thigh pressed tight against hers.

Daniel continued to remain unimpressed by everything, as if his sole purpose in life were to put a damper on the entire day, but Bonnie refused to let that happen. She was too conscious of the brief time left with Russ to allow a spoiled little boy to ruin it.

At noon they enjoyed a lunch of hot dogs, and Bonnie insisted on completing the meal with a cotton candy, her third of the day. While they were finishing up, they spotted Beau and Carolyn, the twins in their double stroller.

"Caro!" Bonnie waved to her sister, trying to catch her attention.

Carolyn waved back and she and Beau beelined it over to where Bonnie, Russ and Daniel sat. "Ah, I should have known we'd find you near the cotton candy vendor," Carolyn teased.

Bonnie grinned, picking the last piece of the sugary confection off the paper cone and popping it into her mouth. "It's better than vitamins at giving me energy," she replied.

"Ha, don't let her fool you," Russ protested. "She has more energy than any ten people put together."

"And I'm ready to get some more," Bonnie replied, tossing the paper cone into a nearby trash container. She laughed as Russ groaned.

"Daniel, are you having a good time?" Carolyn asked.

He shrugged. "It's all right."

"Daniel is the master of understatement," Bonnie explained. "He's having a ball. I swear he almost smiled twice."

Daniel glowered at Bonnie, obviously not finding her amusing. Bonnie fought the desire to alternately wring his neck and hug him tight. She wasn't sure which would do the most good.

"Where are you all headed now?" Beau asked.

"Whatever it is, I want it to be nice and calm. Unlike Bonnie, I prefer to be certain I won't get sick," Russ said.

The teasing smile he cast Bonnie warmed her from the toes up.

"We were heading toward the Ferris wheel," Carolyn explained, and smiled coaxingly at Bonnie. "I know you don't like to ride it. Maybe I could talk you into sitting with the twins while the rest of us do?"

"Sure," Bonnie instantly agreed. "I know Russ wanted to ride, but I have no desire whatsoever."

"Let's go," Russ agreed.

When they got to the Ferris wheel, Daniel balked at the tall structure, insisting he would wait with Bonnie and the twins while his father rode.

Within minutes, Bonnie was sitting on a bench with Daniel, the twins in their stroller, while Russ, Carolyn and Beau waited in line for their turn.

Daniel studiously ignored Bonnie, although two times in as many minutes she saw him smile at the twins. Brent and Trent giggled and cooed at him, each vying for his attention.

"They like you," she observed.

"Who cares," he replied, pretending to ignore the boys.

"I think you do." She studied him thoughtfully. "You work real hard to make people not like you, don't you? Why is that?"

He looked at her sharply, then stared at the ground. "I'm just a bad kid, and I don't care if people like me or not." He raised his chin and eyed her defiantly.

Suddenly Bonnie had a mental vision of herself at that age. She remembered the anger, the pain when she'd first realized her parents didn't have time for her, would never have time for her.

For years she had believed it was her fault. If only she was better behaved, didn't cause problems, then they would love her. She worked harder at being good, and when she saw that didn't change things, she worked hard at being bad. She looked at Daniel again, a new understanding of his attitude dawning.

Leaning against the back of the bench, she fought the impulse to reach out and enfold Daniel in an embrace so tight it would erase all the pain he had inside. "You're lucky," she said.

He peered at her curiously. "Lucky?"

She nodded. "You have a dad who is going to love you no matter how bad you are. He loves you unconditionally. Know what that means?" He shook his head. "That means there is nothing in this world you could do that would make him stop loving you."

Daniel was silent for a few minutes, as if digesting this information. "He might leave me."

"Nope. It would never happen. He'd rather cut off both his arms than leave you." Bonnie grinned. "And what kind of a cop would he make without his arms? He'd have to draw his gun with his toes."

Daniel giggled and Bonnie embraced the sound, so rare, so precious.

He sobered. "My mom left me." The words were barely audible.

"Yeah, she made a really big mistake, and some-day she might realize that. It's amazing, isn't it, that grown-ups can be mixed up and do dumb things?"

Once more she was aware of Daniel's stunned gaze on her, as if he'd never thought about it before. "But I'll bet you were a good kid before your mom left," she continued. "And I'll bet your mom leaving really had nothing at all to do with you. Maybe she was just mixed up and someday she'll be sorry she made such a mistake. You should just feel lucky that you have a dad who will never, ever make that kind of a mis-take."

His brown eyes, so like Russ's, searched her face. "Did your mom and dad love you unditionally?"

Bonnie smiled at his mispronunciation, the smile fleeting as she shook her head. "No, Daniel, they didn't, and that's why I think you are a very lucky lit-tle boy."

Daniel nodded slowly, thoughtfully, then grinned and pointed up to where Russ, Carolyn and Beau had just peaked the Ferris wheel ride. All three of them waved, but it was Russ's face that Bonnie focused on. As he waved down to his son and to Bonnie, she could see his wide smile.

She fought a sudden sting of tears, remembering that in just a matter of days she would leave and probably never see him again. She would never hear his warm laughter, never taste his hot kisses once she had gone. Pain rocked through her, but she knew it was minimal compared with the one she would suffer if she stayed.

Again she reminded herself that no matter how hard she tried, she could never be the kind of woman he deserved, the kind of woman he and Daniel needed in their lives. He was a Ferris wheel, and she was a roller coaster. He was a briefs kind of guy, and she was a boxers kind of woman.

"And never the twain shall meet," she muttered.

"Huh?" Daniel looked at her.

"Never mind." She smiled and stood up. "Come on, let's head over to where the Ferris wheel riders exit. They're getting off now."

When twilight moved in and the carnival lights went on, decorating the darkening sky in brilliant colors, they decided to call it a day. The ride home was quiet, exhaustion replacing the need for conversation.

Bonnie leaned her head back and closed her eyes. She could smell Russ's cologne, the slightly spicy scent she'd come to identify as his alone. She could also smell Daniel, the boyish scent of sun-kissed hair and clean sweat. It was not unpleasant; rather, it wrapped itself around her heart and squeezed gently, reminding her of all she would leave behind.

"Penny for your thoughts," Russ said.

Opening her eyes, she smiled. "You didn't think they were worth much before, so you don't get them now."

Russ sighed in frustration. All day long he'd watched her, as always wondering what was going on in her crazy thoughts, and as always wondering why he cared.

He pulled up before Carolyn and Beau's house, reluctant to call an end to the fun, knowing his time with her was limited. But Daniel was tired and it had been a full day.

"I'll walk you to the door," he said as he turned off the engine.

"That's not necessary," she protested, and was out of the car before he could object. She waved gaily, then disappeared into the house.

Russ swallowed disappointment and restarted the car. He'd wanted to walk her to the door, had hoped to steal a taste of her lips. He'd wanted to kiss her all day, but had never gotten the opportunity.

"Dad?"

"Yes, sport?" He pulled his thoughts away from Bonnie and focused on his son in the back seat.

"Sometimes grown-ups do dumb things, don't they?"

Russ looked at his son in the rearview mirror, surprised by the question. "Sure, I guess they do."

"Mom was dumb to leave me, but you'll never go away 'cause you love me unditionally, right?"

"Right, son." Russ's heart squeezed in his chest. He'd been patiently waiting for Daniel to work through Anne's abandonment, and now it seemed as if Daniel was doing just that. "No matter what you do, how bad you are, I'll always, always love you."

"Yeah, that's what Bonnie said."

Again Russ's gaze went to the rearview mirror. "She did? When did she say that?"

"When you guys were riding on the Ferris wheel."

Daniel was silent and Russ marveled at the fact that whatever Bonnie had said to Daniel had apparently helped the boy deal with some issues that needed to be dealt with.

"Dad?" Daniel leaned forward as far as his seat belt would allow. "I'm sorry I've been sort of bad lately. I've been kind of mad, and kind of sad, but Bonnie said it's not my fault Mom is mixed up."

"I told you that when she first left," Russ replied.

Daniel grinned. "I know, but you're my dad. You're supposed to say junk like that." He was silent for another moment. "Bonnie told me her mom and dad didn't love her unditionally. That's sad, isn't it."

"Yes, it is." Russ was surprised by the peculiar pang in his heart for Bonnie.

For a moment the two males rode in silence, each occupied with his own thoughts.

"Dad?" Daniel broke the silence.

"What, Son?"

"I just wanted to tell you that I love you."

For a moment Russ's vision blurred as his eyes filled with tears. "I love you, too, Son," he finally managed to answer. For the first time, Russ realized he didn't want to say goodbye to Bonnie. He was in love with her...unditionally.

Chapter Ten

"Bonnie! Bonnie wait up," Russ yelled after her as she left the station for the day. He hurried to where she'd paused, her foot tapping impatiently on the sidewalk. The hot pavement shimmered in the mid-August heat. "You heading home?"

She nodded. "I'm going to sit in front of a fan with a glass of iced tea and pretend it isn't as hot as Hades."

"I heard you gave notice today."

"Yeah, Friday will be my last day," she answered, pleased her voice remained unemotional, despite the lump that threatened to form in her throat. She swallowed resolutely.

She'd received her check from Garrison the day before. Her ticket to freedom. Her means of escape. "I haven't seen much of you at the station all week," she observed. "Brenda Jo tells me the carnival is keeping you busy."

He shook his head, the sun stroking rich highlights into its thickness. "I've spent more time out there than I have anywhere else in the past couple of days. There's something about the carnival atmosphere that brings out the bad side of some people."

She clenched her hands at her sides, fighting the desire to rake them through his hair, pull his face closer to hers and fall into the luxury of a kiss. Stop it, she commanded herself. "In another week the carnival will move on and things will get back to normal," she replied.

And in another week she would be gone, off to live the high life, where nobody cared too deeply and saying goodbye didn't hurt. She'd once again embrace the shallow, meaningless life she'd lived before coming to Casey's Corners. "Well, I'd better get home. Carolyn will be expecting me." She turned to leave.

"Bonnie?"

She turned back to look at him, hoping, praying, he would think the shine in her eyes was from the brightness of the sun. "If I were to ask you to stay in Casey's Corners, would you consider it?"

Her chest tightened at his words. "Like you'd ask me to stay," she said with forced flippancy.

"Like you'd stay," he returned.

For a moment he appeared angry, and a yawning hollowness ached in Bonnie's chest. This wasn't a game any longer, and it wasn't fun.

This time when she turned and walked away, he didn't stop her. "Damn, damn, damn!" Bonnie swiped angrily at the tears that trickled down her cheeks. Why hadn't she left before her heart had become so involved? Why hadn't she run before the hurt had begun?

She'd always been so good at escaping her feelings, drowning her pain in frivolous pleasures and exciting adventures. But she had a feeling this particular heartache would be difficult to hide from, impossible to get past.

The moment she received the check, she should have packed up and left, stolen away like a thief in the night. She should have never promised Brenda Jo she'd stay until the end of the week.

Having to see Russ the next couple of days would be sheer torture. His image was burned into her brain—the dancing brown of his eyes, the provocative cleft in his strong chin, those lips that made her feel so desirable. Drat him for making her fall in love with him.

Why had he asked her if she'd consider staying in Casey's Corners? She frowned thoughtfully. Did he want to complete the lovemaking they hadn't finished? Probably. And even if he felt more for her than just physical lust, it didn't matter. She simply loved

Russ too much to attempt any kind of long-term relationship with him.

By the time she got back to her sister's house, she had her emotions firmly under control.

"Did you have a good day?" Carolyn greeted her in the kitchen, where she was busy fixing dinner.

"It was all right," Bonnie said. "Although the air conditioning at the station is on the blink. So we all suffered the heat the entire day." A smile curved her lips as Trent and Brent teetered across the floor to her, hands outstretched in welcome. She got down on her knees and opened her arms to them, laughing as they slobbered kisses on her cheeks and babbled as if telling her about their day.

"They're going to miss you," Carolyn said.

Again Bonnie's heart squeezed convulsively. She nodded and embraced the two little boys, hiding her face in the sweet hollow of Brent's neck. Oh, she was going to miss them, too. They would hold a piece of her heart when she went away. By the time she left there would be so many pieces of her heart in Casey's Corners, she wondered if any of her heart would remain for her to take with her.

Giving the boys each a final kiss, she stood up. "Is there anything I can do to help with dinner?"

Carolyn shook her head. "No, I've got it all under control. The chicken and wild rice is in the oven baking, the salad is in the refrigerator and the green beans are warming on the stove. How about a glass of wine before Beau gets home and we eat?''

"How about a whole bottle of wine?" Bonnie countered, half serious.

"Having second thoughts about leaving?" Carolyn asked.

Bonnie was surprised at her astuteness. "No. I have to leave." She murmured her thanks as Carolyn poured her a glass of white wine. "I have no other choice."

Carolyn poured one for herself, then joined Bonnie at the table. "Why do you have to leave? Why can't you stay here? Make a life for yourself here?"

"I just can't." Bonnie took a sip of the wine, wishing the cool, dry taste could wash away the taste of grief. She stared at Carolyn for a long moment. "I'm in love with Russ." The words escaped from her without her knowing she was going to say them. She instantly regretted them. She'd hoped to escape without anyone discovering what was in her heart.

"I suspected as much," Carolyn said, unsurprised by Bonnie's pronouncement. "But why do you have to leave? Do you know how Russ feels about you?"

"It doesn't matter."

"What do you mean, it doesn't matter?" Carolyn exclaimed, her eyes darkening in confusion.

"Even if he loved me, I couldn't stay...wouldn't stay." Bonnie took another sip of her wine, aware of

Carolyn's perplexed stare. "Caro...face it. What kind of a wife could I be? What kind of a mother would I make?" She forced a light laugh. "I'd screw it all up." She swallowed hard. "I always screw everything up."

"Bonnie, look behind you."

Bonnie frowned. "What?"

"Look behind you," Carolyn demanded. Bonnie turned, gazed around in confusion, then back at her sister. "Bonnie, nobody is there. Nobody is chasing you. Nobody is making you run." Carolyn sighed in frustration. "Oh, Bonnie, I wasted so much of my life trying to be what Father thought I should be. I hate seeing you do the same thing."

"I'm not wasting time trying to be what Father wanted me to be," Bonnie protested.

"No, you're spinning your wheels being exactly what Father said you were for years." Carolyn reached out for Bonnie's hands and gripped them. "He was wrong, Bonnie, and now he's gone. If you love Russ, tell him. Get on with your life. Take control of your happiness."

"You just don't understand," Bonnie protested. She drained her wineglass and stood up. "Do I have time for a walk before dinner?"

Carolyn nodded, still troubled. "But, honey, you can't walk fast enough to escape what's in your heart."

Bonnie didn't reply. None was necessary. With a small wave, she left the house and started up the sidewalk. She had no destination in mind, only a need to walk off the ache in her heart and the confusion Carolyn had stirred.

Carolyn just didn't understand, couldn't relate to, the fear that boiled inside Bonnie at the thought of reaching out to Russ. What if she told him she loved him and he laughed? What if she told him she loved him and he didn't laugh? She didn't know which would be worse. Ultimately she refused to risk it; she had to leave town.

Drawing in a deep breath, Bonnie picked up her pace even though she knew Carolyn was right: she couldn't outrun her heartache.

Russ walked into the station and plopped down at his desk, frowning at the mound of paperwork that awaited him. He looked at his watch. Just after eight o'clock. Within an hour all the businesses along Main Street would be closing down for the night, and the streets would empty as well. He eyed the paperwork again. He really should try to tackle some of it while things were quiet.

Searching for a pencil, he pulled out the top drawer of the metal desk. Finding nothing to write with, he opened the next drawer, frowning as he spied the pieces of the broken figurine Bonnie had bought with her first paycheck. He'd meant to get her another one and had forgotten all about it.

Picking up the fragments, he wondered how much time she had spent shopping for that particular item. It looked like Beau and Carolyn, had obviously been chosen with thought and love.

His heart thudded in sudden apprehension. He loved her, and he couldn't let her leave town without at least telling her what was in his heart. He looked at his watch once again, knowing the next two hours would be agony. He didn't want to wait until tomorrow to tell her how he felt. It was bad enough he had to wait until he got off duty.

Just as he'd suspected, the next two hours crept by. Concentrating was next to impossible unless he concentrated on Bonnie. She filled his heart, pervaded his soul. When he had first met her he hadn't been able to imagine a life with her. Now he could not imagine himself without her.

He jumped up from his desk the minute his replacement deputy appeared. Grabbing his car keys, he waved a quick goodbye and headed out the door.

As he drove to the Randolf house, he tried to imagine how Bonnie would respond to his avowal of love. It was impossible to conjure up her reaction. If he was around her for fifty years, he had a feeling he wouldn't be able to read her mind. But somehow that only made him love her more.

He parked in front of Carolyn and Beau's house, disappointed to see the house dark; everyone was apparently already in bed. He turned off the engine, trying to decide what to do. He didn't want to disturb Beau and Carolyn, nor did he want to put off talking to Bonnie until tomorrow. Now that he had decided to tell her he loved her, he didn't want to wait another minute.

Conceiving of a way to get around bothering Beau and Carolyn, he got out of his car and approached Bonnie's bedroom window. He just hoped she didn't mistake him for another burglar and stick him with a butcher knife. He could just see the headlines of the morning paper: Deputy Gasps Final Words Of Love To Lover Who Stabbed Him. Oh, the town gossips would have a field day.

He hesitated outside the window, wondering if he was about to make a total fool of himself. It didn't matter. Better a fool who tried than a fool who didn't. The window was open, and he wasn't sure if he could actually smell her spicy perfume wafting out or if it was just his imagination.

"Bonnie?" he whispered through the screen. He heard a swift intake of breath, then the rustle of bed sheets.

"Russ?" She appeared at the window, her hair tousled. "What are you doing out there?"

"I need to talk to you. Will you come out?" He held his breath, wondering what he would do if she said no. He needn't have worried.

"Meet me at the back door," she said, then disappeared from his sight.

Russ moved cautiously around the side of the house. Just as he hadn't wanted Bonnie to think him a burglar, he wasn't eager for Beau to make the same mistake and confront him with a gun. He reached the back door and waited, fear and hope creating a nervous jumble inside him.

She came out of the back door, a vision in her blue silk nightgown and matching robe.

"Is something wrong?" she asked worriedly as she quietly closed the door behind her.

The moonlight was full, stroking her face with its silvery hues. Her eyes were luminous and he thought she had never looked lovelier. For a moment his tongue twisted and the words he longed to speak were trapped inside.

"Russ?" Her hand reached up to her throat. "Is...is it about Sam? Have you heard something else?"

Realizing he was frightening her, he quickly shook his head. "No, it's nothing like that. This is about you...about us."

"About us?" She frowned, taking a step away from him.

"Bonnie, I don't know how it happened—I can't tell you when it happened—but somehow I've fallen in love with you."

She stared at him in horror, and for one terrible moment Russ thought she was going to press her hands over her ears to block out his words.

"You're mistaken," she said flatly, not looking at him.

"I'm not mistaken." He took her by the shoulders, but still she refused to meet his gaze. "Listen to me carefully. I am hopelessly, desperately, in love with you." He caressed the silk material at her shoulders. "Don't leave Casey's Corners. Stay and share my life...be my wife."

She raised her face and gazed at him, and in her eyes he saw his love reflected back to him. It was there only a moment, then gone, replaced by brittle amusement.

"Russ, honey, you're mistaking a good old-fashioned case of lust for love." She reached up and patted his cheek. "Don't worry. Lust is sort of like the flu—eventually it will pass."

He grabbed her hand. It was cold, and trembled slightly. "Bonnie, don't do this. Don't try to belittle my love. It's real, and it's not going to go away. I love you, Bonnie. Nothing is going to change that."

"And nothing is going to change the fact that I'm leaving Casey's Corners." Again the dullness was back in her voice and her eyes wouldn't meet his.

"Tell me you don't love me," he demanded. "Look me in the eyes and tell me you don't love me."

She twisted out of his grasp and stepped away from him. "It doesn't matter," she cried. "It doesn't matter whether I love you or not. Russ, we're too different. We'd end up hating each other before all was said and done. I'm not wife material. I'm not mother material." She turned back toward the house. "I've got to go."

Once again Russ stopped her, refusing to let her walk away from him, walk away from his love. "The wife I want is a woman who is unselfish enough to buy a present for her sister and brother-in-law with her first paycheck. The woman I want to spend the rest of my life with is strong enough to go to a funeral home to identify the body of her brother, and she knew just the right words to say to a hurting little boy." He swiped a hand through his hair in frustration. "Bonnie, stop running. Isn't it enough that your brother is on the run? Stay here... make a life with me, with Daniel."

Her eyes shimmered with the burden of unshed tears. "I can't, Russ. Don't you understand? I'd only let you down. You're a briefs kind of guy and I'm a boxers kind of woman." There was a solid finality in her tone.

Russ's heart thunked to the pit of his stomach and pain turned to anger. "Okay, Bonnie...run away and keep on running. But let me tell you something. You are a fake." His words were clipped, concise with the anger and frustration that boiled inside him. "You pretend to be an adventuress, but you're walking away from the biggest adventure of your life." He reached out and wrapped her in his arms, not giving her time to protest.

Instead he claimed her mouth in a fiery kiss that left no doubt of his love. It was a hungry kiss, demanding response, and for a moment she reciprocated, her mouth opening in sweet surrender.

With a tearful groan, she pulled away from him. "Goodbye, Russ," she whispered, then raced to the back door and flew inside.

"Damn!" Russ exploded, fighting the impulse to bang on the door and insist she come out again. Surely if he talked long enough, hard enough she would realize they belonged together. He expelled another sigh of frustration. To hell with it. To hell with her. If she could live with the heartache, so could he.

By Friday morning, Russ realized he was only fooling himself. He couldn't live with the heartache. He didn't want to live without Bonnie. He sat at the kitchen table, watching dawn break over the horizon, knowing that today was the day Bonnie would walk out of his life forever.

The past couple of days had been strained between the two of them. They'd barely spoken and when they had it had been in the tones of polite strangers. Russ had wanted to scream at her, curse her...somehow force her to stay.

He turned as Daniel stumbled into the room. "Hey, sport, what are you doing up so early?" he asked.

Daniel shrugged and slid into the seat across from Russ. "I just woke up and decided to get a drink of water." He eyed Russ curiously. "What are you doing up so early?"

"Just thinking." Russ got up and refilled his coffee cup, then sat back down at the table.

"Thinking about what?"

"Oh, stuff," Russ answered vaguely.

"Love stuff?"

Russ looked at his son in surprise. "Maybe. How did you know that's what I'm thinking about?"

"Mrs. Garfield said you were having love trouble with Bonnie." Daniel tilted his head quizzically. "Do you love her?"

Russ sighed, realizing the town gossips had been busy—he and Bonnie were obviously an interesting topic. "Yes, I do," he answered his son honestly.

"Are we gonna marry her?"

Again Russ gazed at Daniel in surprise. "Do you like her?"

"Sure. She's okay...for a girl."

Russ knew it was the highest compliment his son could make. "No, Daniel, it looks like we aren't gonna

marry her," he answered, irritated at the despair that
rang hollowly in his own voice.

"How come?"

Sighing in frustration, Russ raked a hand through
his hair. "I want to, but I think Bonnie is afraid." He
stared thoughtfully at his son. "She's afraid we'll get
married and somehow I'll stop loving her, I'll leave
her."

"Doesn't she know you love her unditionally?"

Russ gazed back out the window, where the sun now
appeared fully above the horizon. Time was wasting.
She would be up soon, packing her bags, getting ready
to leave. "I don't know, sport. Maybe she needs to
hear it one more time."

He knew she loved him. He knew it from the way
she looked at him, the way she responded to his touch,
his kiss. So why was she turning her back on her feelings? Knowing he had to do something, he jumped up
and went to the telephone, quickly asking Mrs. Garfield if she could sit with Daniel for a little while. As
he hung up, a plan began to formulate in his head.
Bonnie wanted a wild and crazy boxers man. That's
exactly what he intended to give her.

Bonnie stood at her bedroom window, watching the
sunrise. Sleep had been nearly impossible the past few
nights and her heart was heavy as she realized this

would be the last time she would watch the sun shine on Casey's Corners.

Oh, eventually she might return to visit Carolyn and Beau and her two beautiful nephews, but it would never be the same.

The next time she came Russ would be married to some sweet, inoffensive woman who would smell of lavender and never cause him regret. Her heart ached at the very thought.

Heaving a deep sigh, she turned back to the suitcase opened on the bed. Only a few more items and she'd be done. She still hadn't decided where she was going; she knew only that it would be to a place that didn't look like Kansas, couldn't remind her of Russ.

"Bonnie? I think you'd better come out here," Carolyn called from the living room.

Bonnie placed the last blouse in the suitcase and slammed it shut, then went into the living room, where Carolyn stood peering out the front window. "What's going on?" she asked curiously.

Carolyn turned and smiled, her eyes twinkling brightly. "I can't explain it. You'll have to see it to believe it."

Bonnie moved to stand next to her sister and peeked out the window. Shock rippled through her at the spectacle that greeted her. Striding up the street, followed by a growing number of townspeople and clad only in a pair of purple polka-dotted boxers, was Russ.

For a moment her shock kept her rooted to the spot, her gaze drinking in the beauty of his tanned, bare chest, the firm muscular legs. Even in the ridiculous boxers, he was a hunk. He stopped in the middle of the front yard, the crowd of followers stopping at the edge of the sidewalk.

"Bonnie Baker." His voice reverberated in the sudden stillness. "You wanted a wild and crazy boxers man. You've got one. I'm wild and crazy in love with you."

The crowd cheered and began to chant, "Bonnie. Bonnie. Bonnie." Their voices filled the air like crazed fans at a music concert.

"You'd better get out there before that mob comes in and carries you out."

Carolyn's words broke Bonnie's inertia. She raced to the front door, threw it open and motioned Russ inside, refusing to acknowledge the hopeful beating of her heart. Nothing has changed, she reminded herself. Her bags were packed and she was ready to leave. Russ standing in the front yard half-naked changed nothing.

Russ came inside, the look in his eyes as wild and crazy as the boxers he wore. As if by magic, Carolyn disappeared from the room, leaving Russ and Bonnie to face each other alone.

"Do you really think this will change my mind?" Bonnie asked.

Russ shrugged. "At this point I'm willing to do whatever it takes to keep you here and in my life."

His gaze caressed her lovingly, causing her heart to ache painfully.

Bonnie ignored the hurt, wishing he wouldn't make this more difficult than it already was. "Russ, it just wouldn't work. I'd do something stupid. I'd embarrass you, disappoint you, and eventually you'd be sorry you ever married me."

"You've forgotten one very important fact." He moved closer to her, his eyes the warm brown of rich earth.

"I told you once that when I love, I love unconditionally. There is nothing in this world you could do to make me stop loving you."

The words seeped inside her, warming her and promising the kind of love and acceptance she'd always sought. She saw the love, the promise, in his eyes. She wanted to reach out to him, embrace his love... but she was so afraid. She closed her eyes, seeking the strength to walk away from him. Why was he making it all so hard? "I can't cook," she finally said.

"I can."

He wrapped his arms around her, his bare skin smelling of his cologne and the fresh scent of sunshine.

"I might decide one day to go skinny-dipping in a pond," she returned.

"I'll just go with you." He smiled at her, a smile full of love, rife with passion. "Unconditionally, Bonnie Baker. I love you and nothing you could ever do will change that fact. I want you to be my wife, and I'll follow you around the country in horrid-looking boxers if that's what it takes to make you mine."

Bonnie laughed, and in her laughter was release from her fear. She believed him. Tears sparkled in her eyes as she gazed at his face. "Oh, Russ, I love you, and I want to spend the rest of my life with you and Daniel."

Joy danced on his face, and with a groan he claimed her lips, kissing her deeply, thoroughly. When they parted, Bonnie leaned her cheek against the warmth of his chest, nuzzling against his sweet-smelling skin.

"As if I could ever leave you," he murmured into her hair.

"As if I'd let you." She raised her head and grinned at him. Together they laughed, and as they kissed once again, Bonnie knew her days of running were over. She had found what she sought—herself, her life, her love—with Russ.

Epilogue

Bonnie stood in front of the mirror, staring at her reflection in awe. A bride. Today she would marry Russ, and she truly felt that it would be the first day of her life. A real life, with substance and meaning, with love and laughter. "Dreams," she murmured to the woman in the mirror. Today those long-ago dreams were coming true.

It had been a full week since Russ had stalked up the street wearing those ridiculous purple boxers, and in those seven days, Bonnie had only been assured of Russ's love. Even Daniel seemed happy with the idea of her being part of their family. He'd jumped into the wedding plans with both feet, making suggestions and helping Russ choose Bonnie's ring.

She returned her attention to the mirror. The dress she had on wasn't the same one she'd worn when she'd run out on Helmut. Russ had insisted she buy another one and she had agreed. Traditional white, the gown had classical lines and layers of lace, making her look far more angelic than she thought possible.

"Can I come in?" Carolyn's voice drifted through the door.

"Sure."

Carolyn walked in, a vision of loveliness in her gown. The purple dress brought out the blue of her eyes and the color in her cheeks. Bonnie had insisted on purple, having developed a fondness for the bright color since the day of Russ's momentary madness.

"Oh, Bonnie." Tears immediately formed in Carolyn's eyes as she gazed at her sister. "You look absolutely radiant." She crossed the small floor of the church dressing room and hugged Bonnie tight. "I'm so happy for you." She stepped back. "It's a happy day."

Bonnie nodded, for a moment her heart too filled to speak. "I just wish Colleen and Sam could be here. That would have made it a perfect day," she finally managed to say.

Bonnie had tried to get their youngest sister to come out from Long Island for the wedding, but Colleen

was in the middle of testifying at a child-custody
hearing and couldn't get away. As for Sam...

"You know they'd be here if they could," Carolyn
replied softly.

Bonnie looked at her sister, and realized she was
thinking the same thoughts. Would Sam ever come
back and be a part of their lives? Or would he end up
caught by the police, and spend the rest of his life in
prison for a murder they were all certain he didn't
commit? Oh, Sam, Bonnie thought, I wish you could
quit running, the way I have.

Carolyn looked at her watch. "You only have a few
minutes before you walk up that aisle."

Bonnie reached into the small suitcase she had
brought with her to the church. "I have a present for
you," she said.

"Your happiness is all the present I want," Carolyn protested.

"It's just a little something." Bonnie handed Carolyn a jeweler's box. "It's not the same as the one that
was stolen, but it's close," she explained as Carolyn
opened the box to reveal a gold chain necklace with a
phoenix charm. "The charm is a little bigger than the
original, but Father must have had the others spe-
cially made."

"Oh, Bonnie, it's lovely."

Bonnie gazed at the necklace with a small smile.
"Somehow the phoenix seems appropriate for us.

Hopefully all of us can rise out of the ashes of our childhood to find happiness.''

"I just wish I knew why somebody wanted to steal the others.''

"We'll probably never know,'' Bonnie replied. "Caro, would you do me a favor and find Brenda Jo and send her in? I have a little something for her, too.''

"Sure. I'll be right back.'' Carolyn left the room.

A moment later Brenda Jo appeared, her purple gown clashing horrendously with her bright-red hair. She looked at Bonnie and burst into tears. "Oh, sweetie, I'm so happy for you,'' she wailed. She pulled a pink tissue from her bodice and wiped her eyes. "Don't mind me. I always cry at weddings.''

Bonnie gave the older woman a tight hug, then handed her an envelope. "Let's hope the next wedding you cry at is your own.''

Brenda Jo gave her eyes a final swipe and opened the envelope. As she saw the airline tickets inside, she wailed again. The tears streamed down her face as she grabbed Bonnie in a bear hug.

Laughing, Bonnie disentangled herself from the older woman's grasp. "Consider that our wedding present to you and Lloyd. Two round-trip tickets to Paris. Now, you go out there and tell Lloyd there is no reason the two of you can't get married right away.''

"You made my dream come true," Brenda Jo cried, "and all I got you was a Crockpot."

"Everything all right in here?" Carolyn stuck her head inside the room.

"Everything is fine," Bonnie assured her. "Brenda Jo was just leaving to speak to Lloyd."

"Yes...yes, I've got to go talk to that man of mine." Smiling radiantly, Brenda Jo left the room and Carolyn reentered.

"What did you do to her?" Carolyn asked curiously.

Bonnie smiled. "Just made a little dream of hers come true." Her nerves jumped as she heard the chords of the organist. "Is it time?"

Carolyn smiled. "It's time."

Together the two sisters left the little dressing room and joined the others who stood ready to walk down the aisle in the formal procession.

Before Bonnie knew it, the people in the church were on their feet, and it was her turn to walk down the flower-bedecked path. She stood there for a moment, looking at Russ, tall and proud next to the minister.

She waited for the old, familiar unease to ripple through her, for the desire to run away to suffuse her. They didn't come. The fear of disappointing, the fear of not being loved were gone, swallowed up by the loving look in Russ's eyes, the smile that lit Daniel's face.

The only thing she felt was an overwhelming need to run...run as fast as she could toward Russ and her future. Taking a deep breath and picking up her long, lace skirt, that's exactly what she did.

*   *   *   *   *

COMING NEXT MONTH

#1150 WELCOME HOME, DADDY!—Kristin Morgan
Fabulous Fathers
The Murdock marriage was over—or was it? Ross Murdock was
determined to win back his wife, Rachel, especially after discovering another baby was on the way!

#1151 AN UNEXPECTED DELIVERY—Laurie Paige
Bundles of Joy
Talk about labor pains! Any-minute-mom-to-be Stacey Gardenas
was on an assignment when her baby decided to be born. And that
meant her handsome boss, Gareth Clelland, had to help deliver the
child.

#1152 AN IMPROMPTU PROPOSAL—Carla Cassidy
The Baker Brood
Colleen Jensen was desperate—and Gideon Graves was the only
one who could help her. But while searching for Colleen's missing
brother, would Gideon find the way to her heart?

**#1153 THE RANCHER AND THE LOST BRIDE—
Carol Grace**
Parker's sweet little girl made Christine feel like part of the fami-
ly—as did the sparks between her and the rugged rancher!
But could forgotten memories keep Christine from being a *true*
family member?

#1154 AND MOMMY MAKES THREE—Lynn Bulock
Long ago, Matt Viviano gave up on love and happy endings. But
the way Larissa Camden lit up his son's face was a dream come true,
and if Matt wasn't careful, he'd find himself in his own storybook
romance.

#1155 FAMILY MINE—Elizabeth Krueger
Marriage? Meredith Blackmoore refused to even *consider* marrying
Stoney Macreay. She could not ignore her daughter's wish for a
father and Stoney's desire for a family, but could she resist *her* own
need for Stoney?

MILLION DOLLAR SWEEPSTAKES
AND EXTRA BONUS PRIZE DRAWING

No purchase necessary. To enter the sweepstakes, follow the directions published and complete and mail your Official Entry Form. If your Official Entry Form is missing, or you wish to obtain an additional one (limit: one Official Entry Form per request, one request per outer mailing envelope) send a separate, stamped, self-addressed #10 envelope (4 1/8" x 9 1/2") via first class mail to: Million Dollar Sweepstakes and Extra Bonus Prize Drawing Entry Form, P.O. Box 1867, Buffalo, NY 14269-1867. Request must be received no later than January 15, 1998. For eligibility into the sweepstakes, entries must be received no later than March 31, 1998. No liability is assumed for printing errors, lost, late, non-delivered or misdirected entries. Odds of winning are determined by the number of eligible entries distributed and received.

Sweepstakes open to residents of the U.S. (except Puerto Rico), Canada and Europe who are 18 years of age or older. All applicable laws and regulations apply. Sweepstakes offer void wherever prohibited by law. Values of all prizes are in U.S. currency. This sweepstakes is presented by Torstar Corp., its subsidiaries and affiliates, in conjunction with book, merchandise and/or product offerings. For a copy of the Official Rules governing this sweepstakes, send a self-addressed, stamped envelope (WA residents need not affix return postage) to: MILLION DOLLAR SWEEP-STAKES AND EXTRA BONUS PRIZE DRAWING Rules, P.O. Box 4470, Blair, NE 68009-4470, USA.

SWP-ME96

"Motherhood is full of love, laughter
and sweet surprises. Silhouette's collection
is every bit as much fun!"
—Bestselling author Ann Major

This May, treat yourself to...

WANTED:

MOTHER

Silhouette's annual tribute to motherhood takes a
new twist in '96 as three sexy single men prepare for
fatherhood—and saying "I Do!" This collection makes
the perfect gift, not just for moms but for all romance
fiction lovers! Written by these captivating authors:

Annette Broadrick
Ginna Gray
Raye Morgan

BOOKS

THE
GREATEST
GIFT

"The Mother's Day anthology from Silhouette is the
highlight of any romance lover's spring!"
—Award-winning author **Dallas Schulze**

Silhouette®

™

MD96

As seen on TV!
Free Gift Offer

With a Free Gift proof-of-purchase from any Silhouette® book,
you can receive a beautiful cubic zirconia pendant.

This gorgeous marquise-shaped stone is a genuine cubic
zirconia—accented by an 18" gold tone necklace.

(Approximate retail value $19.95)

Send for yours today...
compliments of ▼ *Silhouette*®
TM

To receive your free gift, a cubic zirconia pendant, send us one original proof-of-
purchase, photocopies not accepted, from the back of any Silhouette Romance™,
Silhouette Desire®, Silhouette Special Edition®, Silhouette Intimate Moments®
or Silhouette Shadows™ title available in February, March or April at your favorite
retail outlet, together with the Free Gift Certificate, plus a check or money order for
$1.75 U.S./$2.25 CAN. (do not send cash) to cover postage and handling, payable
to Silhouette Free Gift Offer. We will send you the specified gift. Allow 6 to 8 weeks for
delivery. Offer good until April 30, 1996 or while quantities last. Offer valid in the U.S. and
Canada only.

Free Gift Certificate

Name: _____

Address: _____

City: _____ State/Province: _____ Zip/Postal Code: _____

Mail this certificate, one proof-of-purchase and a check or money order for postage
and handling to: SILHOUETTE FREE GIFT OFFER 1996. In the U.S.: 3010 Walden
Avenue, P.O. Box 9057, Buffalo NY 14269-9057. In Canada: P.O. Box 622, Fort Erie,

---

FREE GIFT OFFER   079-KBZ-R
ONE PROOF-OF-PURCHASE
To collect your fabulous FREE GIFT, a cubic zirconia pendant, you must include this
original proof-of-purchase for each gift with the properly completed Free Gift Certificate.

079-KBZ-R

You're About to Become a *Privileged Woman*

Reap the rewards of fabulous free gifts and
benefits with proofs-of-purchase from
Silhouette and Harlequin books

Pages & Privileges™

It's our way of thanking you for
buying our books at your
favorite retail stores.

PROOF OF
PURCHASE
Offer expires October 31, 1996

SR-PP124

Harlequin and Silhouette—
the most privileged readers in the world!

For more information about Harlequin and
Silhouette's PAGES & PRIVILEGES program call the
Pages & Privileges Benefits Desk: 1-503-794-2499

Silhouette®

SR-PP124